6
A DIXIE MORRIS ANIMAL ADVENTURE

GILBERT MORRIS

MOODY PRESS
CHICAGO

26677

All Scripture quotations, unless indicated, are taken from the
New American Standard Bible, © 1960, 1962, 1963, 1968,
1971, 1972, 1973, 1975, 1977, and 1994 by The Lockman
Foundation, La Habra, Calif. Used by permission.

ISBN: 0-8024-3368-5

1 3 5 7 9 10 8 6 4 2

Printed in the United States of America

*To Ms Nan—
Thank you for all the
fun times you have
given me!
I love you so much!
Dixie Lynn*

CONTENTS

1.	Dixie Gets a Call	7
2.	The Raccoon	17
3.	Birthday Party	31
4.	Barbie Dolls	43
5.	Dixie Loses Her Temper	55
6.	A Bad Guy	69
7.	The Master Plan	79
8.	A Startling Development	93
9.	Coon Trouble	105
10.	Dixie Decides	121
11.	Trouble for Bandit and Company	129
12.	To the Rescue	143

1
DIXIE
GETS A CALL

Dixie Morris moved among the racks of summer clothing, considering what would look best on her. She had tried on a pair of Levi's and a cranberry-colored blouse and now gazed at herself in the mirror again. The reflection she saw was of a very pretty eleven-year-old girl with blue eyes and long blonde hair. She was small, almost petite. She decided the outfit was just what she wanted.

"Dixie, you've looked at everything in the store!" the woman behind her said. Sarah Logan was a tall woman with red hair and green eyes. She shook her head, adding, "We've got to be on our way! We can't shop for the rest of our lives!"

"All right, Aunt Sarah. I'll go change back." Dixie went into the dressing room, quickly changed, and came out with the jeans and blouse in her hand. She also chose a pair of Keds. As the saleslady smiled at her, Dixie said, "This will be all for today."

"You made some good choices. It looks like you've had a lot of experience shopping."

"She certainly has." Aunt Sarah was tapping her toe impatiently. She was wearing a pair of white shorts today, a blue T-shirt, and a pair of white tennis shoes. She did not look like the veterinarian for the exotic animals of the Royal Circus, but that was what she was.

"Come *on,* Dixie! It'll be time for supper soon, and I'm starved!"

The two drove quickly through the city and came to where the circus was located on the edge of town. When they were inside their trailer, Dixie announced, "I'm going to cook supper tonight, Aunt Sarah!"

Her aunt smiled. "That's fine, Dixie. You're getting to be a real good cook. What are we going to have?"

"Spaghetti!"

It was her favorite.

"That's good! You do very well with

spaghetti. I'll go do some of my book work, and afterwards we can watch television for a while."

"All right."

Dixie busied herself around the small kitchen. At first, she had had difficulty adjusting to the fact that kitchens in trailers were small like everything else. But she knew where everything was and began getting together the ingredients for supper. She took the hamburger meat from the refrigerator and added chopped onions and bell peppers. Stirring in tomato sauce and spaghetti sauce mix, she quickly had the meat prepared, and soon it was browning.

She filled a saucepan with water then and, when it began to boil, added the spaghetti. She always liked that part—poking down the stiff, long, skinny pieces of pasta, for as they hit the water they suddenly became as flexible as rubber. She cooked the spaghetti until it was tender, then poured it into a drainer.

"You'd better hurry up, Aunt Sarah! I'm almost through!" she called.

"All right! I'll set the table!"

When the two sat down, Dixie said, "I'll ask the blessing." Without waiting further, she bowed her head and began to pray. "Lord, we thank You for this spaghetti. We know that all our food comes from You, every bite we have. Thank You. In Jesus' name."

Aunt Sarah smiled fondly at her niece and began to sprinkle Tabasco sauce over her spaghetti. "What did your parents say in the letter you got this morning?" She had taken Dixie to live with her while Dixie's parents were on a mission assignment in Africa. The two had become fast friends.

But Dixie was watching her aunt put the hot sauce on her spaghetti. She shuddered. "I don't see how you can eat that! It kills all the taste!" But she had had this argument with her aunt before and now gave it up. "Dad and Mom said there may be a chance they'll get to move to a new place, and then I can come and live with them."

"You'd like that, wouldn't you?" Sarah was rolling her spaghetti around her fork before taking a bite of it. "I know you get lonesome for them."

"I sure do, but it's fun living with you. And not every girl gets to be in a circus parade and be around all the wonderful animals." Dixie took a bite and turned her head to one side. A smile turned up her lips, and she said, "I'd miss Stripes if I was anywhere else." Stripes. The huge Siberian tiger that she had grown very fond of since coming to live with the Royal Circus.

They sat at the table talking until, finally, just as Aunt Sarah said, "It's my turn to do the dishes," the phone rang.

"I'll get it," Dixie said quickly. She ran to the phone and, picking it up, said, "Hello?"

"Dixie, is that you?"

"Yes . . . it is . . ." She hesitated for a moment more and then asked, "Is that *you*, Uncle Roy?"

"Yes!" The voice belonged to Roy Snyder, a relative of her father's. Dixie had spent a summer with the Snyders, where she had gotten involved with an African elephant called Jumbo.

"How are you, Uncle Roy?" she asked. "And how's Aunt Edith?"

"Well, I'm all right, but your aunt is not so good. As a matter of fact, she's not good at all."

"What's wrong? Is she sick?"

11

"Well, you know that back porch that I've been threatening to fix for a long time? It finally gave in with her, and she broke her leg real bad."

"Oh, Uncle Roy, I'm sorry to hear that!"

"Well, let me talk to your Aunt Sarah, Dixie."

Dixie looked toward Sarah, who was watching. "It's Uncle Roy. He says Aunt Edith's broken her leg."

"Oh my!" Her aunt flew to the phone, and Dixie stood listening, waiting to find out the details of her aunt's accident. Finally Aunt Sarah said, "I'd love to come and take care of Aunt Edith, but I don't see how I possibly could, Roy. It's a bad time for me to be away from the circus . . ."

Dixie understood what was happening. Her uncle had asked Aunt Sarah to come and help with the care of Aunt Edith. "Aunt Sarah," she said quickly, "*I* could go take care of Aunt Edith."

Sarah looked at her with surprise. "That would be too big a job for you, Dixie!"

"I can do it!" Dixie said quickly. "I can cook, and I could wait on Aunt Edith and make the beds and things. I really ought to do it. They were so nice to me last summer."

Aunt Sarah stared at Dixie a moment and said into the phone, "Roy, I can't come, but Dixie says she could." She listened intently, then said, "All right. I'll see about the reservations. You'll pick her up at the airport?" She listened again. "All right, here she is." Turning to Dixie, she said, "Uncle Roy wants to speak to you, Dixie."

Dixie took the phone. "Yes, Uncle Roy?"

"Dixie, it's real fine of you to offer to come and help. I never thought about *you* coming. But I've got to have *somebody* to help me with your aunt. She won't be able to get around very much for most of the summer, and I just can't afford a full-time nurse."

"Oh, that's all right, Uncle Roy," Dixie said breezily. "I'll be glad to come. I had so much fun with you last summer, and now I'll get to do some fun things again and see some of my friends and help you, too. You just wait! When I get there I'll take care of you and Aunt Edith both!"

"Well, that'll be fine, Dixie. I'll get your

room ready for you, and I'll go tell Aunt Edith. She'll be real glad you're coming. 'Bye now."

"Good-bye, Uncle Roy."

Dixie hung up the phone and turned her head to one side questioningly. "When do I leave, Aunt Sarah?"

"I'll call the airport and find out when the planes leave." Sarah came over then and put her arms around Dixie. Her eyes were warm as she said, "I'm very proud of you. I know it won't all be easy and fun, but at times like this we all have to pull together."

Dixie was pleased with her aunt's approval. "Well, Jumbo won't be there, but I know I'll have fun. I can go fishing in the creek like I did last summer."

"I'm sure you can," Sarah said. She smiled and hugged Dixie again. "Now you start getting your clothes ready, and I'll call the airport."

2
THE RACCOON

Dixie loved to ride in planes, and the big jet that soared far above the earth seemed like a large bird to her. She loved to stare out the window at the fleecy white clouds below.

The flight attendant who came by to bring her lunch smiled down and said, "We're glad to have you with us today. Are you going on a vacation?"

"Oh no. I'm going home to take care of my Aunt Edith." Dixie smiled back. "I've been with the Royal Circus," she announced proudly.

"Really!" The flight attendant was a short young woman with curly blonde hair and large blue eyes. "What did you do in the circus?"

"Well, my aunt is the veterinarian, and

she takes care of all of the animals. But I do an act with a tiger."

"Do you really? You mean you actually get in the cage with him?"

"Yes, let me show you!" Dixie fumbled through her bag, and soon the flight attendant was exclaiming over the pictures.

She held up one where Dixie was wearing a filmy blue silk costume and was astride a huge albino tiger. "Why, it *is* you!" she exclaimed. "I thought you were fooling me!"

"No, and that's Stripes! He's my special favorite." Dixie went on talking excitedly.

Finally the attendant said, "I guess it will be boring for you back home without all the animals."

"Oh, there are lots of animals at my Uncle Roy's place—he has a farm! Of course, there aren't any farm animals as big as a Siberian tiger, though!"

After the attendant moved on to serve the other people, Dixie settled back. The lunch was not very good, she thought, biting into the cold sandwich. *Why, I could do better than this myself!*

Her mind began to leap ahead, and she pictured herself cooking for passengers on an airliner. It was her way of making believe. As soon as that was over, she pretended she was the pilot flying the huge airplane through the sky. At last Dixie dozed off.

She was awakened by the captain's voice saying, "We're now preparing to land! Fasten your safety belts!"

Dixie scrambled around and snapped her belt, then watched as the earth beneath seemed to rush up to meet her. The cars on the highways below looked like toys, and she saw black-and-white cows feeding in a green meadow beside a winding silver river.

And then the wheels touched down, and soon the plane came to a halt. Dixie unfastened her safety belt, hurried to put her books into her carry-on bag, and then got in the line that was filing off the jet.

As soon as she stepped outside, she saw her uncle standing with others behind a fence. She waved, shouting loudly, "Hello, Uncle Roy!"

Her uncle grinned and waved back. He was wearing blue overalls and a white straw hat, as usual, and looked exactly as he always had. He was not a handsome man, being overweight, and his hair had fallen out, leaving his head half bald. Neverthe-

less, she was glad to see him. When she got
to him and he picked her up and spun her
around, she felt very good about being
there.

"I'm sure glad to see you, Dixie!" he
said, putting her down. "I can't tell you how
much we appreciate you coming to help
with the house until your Aunt Edith gets
better."

"I'm glad to be here," Dixie said.

They walked inside the terminal and
waited until her suitcase came out on the
round baggage track. Uncle Roy picked it
up and said, "Let's get on home! Aunt Edith
is dying to see you!"

He put her suitcase in the back of his
black Ford pickup, then got in behind the
wheel. Dixie got in beside him, and then
they were out of the airport and headed toward Cedarville. She at once kept Uncle Roy
busy answering her questions about her
friends and how things were on the farm.

Soon they turned off the main high-
way, and fifteen minutes later they were in
Cedarville. The place brought back good
memories to Dixie. It was just a small town,
but it had a white church with a steeple in
the center of it, and a very wide main street

on which businesses were lined up on both sides.

Uncle Roy and Aunt Edith's house was almost outside the city limits but not quite. Dixie's heart leaped when she saw the familiar house, a two-story white building with a pointed roof and a large red barn out to one side. When she leaped out of the truck, a Border collie, barking excitedly, came at once to jump up and try to lick her face.

"Shep!" Dixie cried. She hugged the dog, who licked her ear enthusiastically. "Get down now, Shep! You're going to get me all dirty!"

"Hello, Dixie!"

Dixie turned to see a very large man with blond hair and mild blue eyes. It was Candy Sweet, the hired hand, and Dixie ran to him.

Candy bent down to give her a hug. "I'm glad to see you," he said very slowly. He never talked much, but he and Dixie had become fast friends during her stay the summer before.

"Are you going to take me fishing down at the creek, Candy?"

"Guess I might as well." He grinned.

He seemed to be trying to think of something else to say. "We got a new calf," he finally told her. "I'll take you to see her as soon you get your bag in the house."

"All right, Candy. You'll have to show me *everything* that's new!"

Dixie left her uncle to bring her suitcase and ran into the house. "Aunt Edith, I'm here!" she cried.

"Dixie, come in the living room!"

Dixie went down the big hallway that divided the lower story into two parts and found her aunt sitting in a wheelchair. Aunt Edith's leg was propped out in front of her and had a huge cast on it.

"Come here and let me hug you!" she cried. She was a thin woman. Her glasses were shoved up on her head. Last summer she'd often lost them, and Dixie had to find them for her. Hugging Dixie awkwardly, Aunt Edith said, "I'm so sorry you had to come and take care of an old woman."

"Don't say that, Aunt Edith!" Dixie said. "I'm happy to, and it'll be fun! I'm just sorry you broke your leg. Does it hurt?"

"Well, not much now, but it's hard for me to get around. Can't sweep the floor, or stand up to cook, or anything else. Don't know how you'll make out doing the washing and ironing. I'm afraid it's a lot for a little girl."

Dixie shook her head. "No, it's not! I'm not *little.* I can do it all! You'll see!"

"Well, we have Cleo come in twice a week to do the heavy cleaning. Mostly, if you can just cook for your uncle and me, that'll be wonderful."

"I've learned to cook a whole lot! I do almost all the cooking for me and Aunt Sarah!"

"Well, your uncle's got a lot of groceries bought. But first, sit down here and tell me all about what you and your aunt have been doing."

Uncle Roy came in then, and Dixie sat and talked a long time with her aunt and uncle. She told them excitedly about Stripes, and of how she had made a pet of a gorilla called Dolly, and then about her trip to the Middle East, where she had become friends with a camel named Sandy.

When she finally stopped, Uncle Roy said with a smile, "I hope you don't find another elephant. That one you found last summer gave us a lot of trouble."

Dixie laughed. "I sure do miss Jumbo,

though. Aunt Sarah says we can go to Arkansas and visit him this summer when she gets here. Now," she said, "I'm going to unpack and then start supper!"

She went upstairs and unpacked her suitcase, looking around with fondness at her room. It was quite large, about ten by twelve, with two big windows covered with pink-and-white-striped cotton curtains. The walls were papered with a light pink-and-white background that had delicate blue-and-yellow flowers running through it. The floor was covered with a rag rug in a multitude of colors. The bed had tall posts on all four corners. A thick white comforter with tiny pink bows lay on the bed, and pillows in all shapes, sizes, and colors stood around the headboard. A simple globe lamp was on the bedside table. The furniture in the room was large and old, but she saw there was also a small TV.

Then she went downstairs and checked the kitchen cupboard. She said aloud, "I think I'll make pasta tonight. And brownies."

After an hour's work, Dixie was sitting at the table with her uncle and aunt, listening with pleasure as both praised the meal. She had opened a can of green beans to go with the pasta. It was all very good, they said. Dixie's specialty was brownies, although she didn't make them from scratch, as she knew Aunt Edith did, but used a box of mix.

As the meal ended, she sat back, eating brownies and drinking milk and feeling surprised at how glad she was to be back. She said, "I've missed you both."

"I'm surprised about that!" Aunt Edith said. "You've led such an exciting life with that circus. Moving around, and all kinds of wild animals—I wouldn't think you'd have time to miss life out on a farm."

"I did, though! Circus life is nice, but there's something good about going to bed in the same place every night. In the circus you might go to bed in Chicago and get up and leave and go to Pittsburgh the next day."

She talked about the circus for a while, then said, "I'll do the dishes."

"I'll help you," Uncle Roy offered.

"No, you go in and read the paper, Uncle Roy! I'll be in as soon as I get through!"

Dixie washed the dishes and wiped the table. Then she went into the large living room, where she found Uncle Roy and Aunt

Edith. She sat and talked with them for a while but was surprised to find that she was very tired.

"I don't know why I'm so tired and sleepy! I haven't done anything except cook one meal and ride on an airplane."

"Maybe it's that jet lag I've heard about," her uncle suggested.

"That's right. You'd better go up and go to bed."

"All right. I think I will." Dixie went over and kissed her aunt and hugged her, saying, "I'm glad I'm able to be here and help, Aunt Edith." She kissed her uncle too, then went upstairs and prepared for bed.

The bathroom in the old house was *very* large. It had not been a bathroom at all at first, just a big room, but her uncle had fixed it up so that now it had a shining white tub with claw feet, and Dixie soaked in the tub for a long time.

When she put on her pajamas, she looked down at them, noticing again that they had Donald Duck's picture all over them. "These are really ugly pajamas!" she said. "I'm going to get me some new ones the next time I go shopping!" She brushed her teeth and flossed, having promised Aunt Sarah she would do this, and then she climbed into bed.

As always, before she went to sleep, Dixie read a chapter in her Bible. It was not exactly like Aunt Sarah's Bible but was called the *Living Bible* and was written in words that she could understand very easily. After she had read her chapter, she said her prayers, then turned out the light and settled down to go to sleep.

She must have gone to sleep almost instantly, but sometime during the night a sound woke her. Perhaps it was because the house was so quiet that she heard it. Back where the trailer was parked at the circus, there were always cars coming, cars going, people shouting, and all kinds of disturbances, even late at night.

She lay for a while, almost going back to sleep, and then she heard it again. This time she sat straight up in bed.

"It may be a burglar!" she whispered. Dixie got out of bed and went to the window. Her room faced the street, and she bent her head trying to see the front porch but couldn't—just the steps.

She crossed to a window that faced the

side of the house, quietly lifted the window, leaned out, and peered into the night. The stars were out, and the moon was a huge silver disk. The yard and the porch were flooded with moonlight.

A movement caught her eye, and she drew in her breath. She could not see what it was, but she stayed at the window a long time, wondering whether or not to get her uncle out of bed. And then she saw it again!

Right under her window, a small form had suddenly climbed down from the porch, and as Dixie watched, she saw that it was a very large raccoon.

Dixie had seen coons before but not one this close. She must have made some noise, for the animal suddenly looked up at her. He was holding something in his paws and had been nibbling on it. She saw his bright eyes and, as always, thought that coons looked like burglars. They seemed to wear black masks.

"Hello, there," she whispered down to him. "What are you doing here?"

The coon did not run away but watched her carefully, continuing to nibble on what-ever it was that he was eating. He looked so much like a burglar that Dixie said, "I think your name ought to be Bandit."

The coon cocked his masked head to one side, then dropped to all fours and scurried to the corner of the house. As he disappeared into some woods at the back, Dixie said, "I'll put out some dog food for you tomorrow. That's what I'll do."

She pulled her head back inside and returned to bed. *Bandit,* she thought sleepily. *Coons are such cute animals with that ringed tail and those little hands and that black mask. The farmers say they steal corn, but they can't help that. I guess they think it's there just for them to eat.*

She turned over and went to sleep and dreamed about raccoons. Not just one, but dozens of raccoons. She was sitting in the middle of them. They were crowded around her, and she was petting them and feeding them. And they all looked alike with their black masks and their little grins, and their tiny raccoon hands were reaching out and touching her.

3

BIRTHDAY PARTY

Three days had passed since Dixie arrived in Cedarville. During that time she had taken over the cooking and much of the housecleaning for her uncle and aunt. It was, indeed, a great deal of fun for her. *I didn't know how busy I really was with the circus,* she thought more than once. *It's so quiet and calm here.*

She certainly slept well, even though each night was broken by the visit she received from Bandit. After her first sighting of the masked intruder, she'd left a dish of dog food and a bowl of water on the front steps—she knew raccoons sometimes liked to wash their food.

Her uncle and aunt usually went to bed early, and on the second night she had been sitting up alone, reading, when she heard a slight noise. She went to the front door and found Bandit, who watched her cautiously.

Dixie slipped out onto the porch, where she stood at a distance and watched him. He returned her gaze and finally resumed eating the dog food.

"You sure are a bold thing," she said.

The next night she had a small bowl of green grapes ready. When Bandit finished the dog food, she squatted down and held out the dish. "Come on, have some dessert," she had said encouragingly.

Bandit had backed away, and Dixie thought at first he intended to leave. But she kept whispering to him and making a clucking noise with her tongue. The coon began to edge closer, eyeing the grapes. Finally he was close enough to thrust out a paw and take one.

"That's right! Help yourself!" Dixie grinned. "And they are good for you!"

The raccoon edged a little closer. This time he sat up. He reached out and with one hand grasped the bowl. With the other he picked out a grape. He put it in his mouth, turned his head upward, and chewed. Then he reached for another.

Dixie laughed softly. She watched the

raccoon eat the whole bowl of grapes, always the same way. She saw that he could pick up a grape as easily as she could herself. "Your paws are just like little hands, Bandit!" she said. "But I wonder why you turn your head *up* to eat."

Bandit merely looked at her, popped a grape into his mouth, then turned his head upward again.

"I know!" Dixie cried. "It's so you won't spill the juice! Isn't that clever!"

Bandit ate all the grapes and then ambled away.

Dixie enjoyed the visit of the coon and wrote about him in her diary.

I have a new friend. His name is Bandit. He's not as big as Stripes or Jumbo, but he's real cute. He has a black mask, and he likes to eat grapes and dog food. I bet if I keep on feeding him, we'll be real friends.

The day after she wrote that, Dixie received a visitor. Sheriff Henry Peck, a tall, black-haired man, stopped by the Snyder house. He grinned down at her and said, "Good to see you back, Dixie."

"How are you, Sheriff Peck?"

"Fine. You ever hear from that fellow Chad Taylor?"

"Oh, all the time! He's doing great, Sheriff!"

Chad had been fifteen last summer. He and Dixie had become great friends while trying to keep Jumbo the elephant hidden from the townspeople.

"Well, I hope you don't dig up any more elephants," the sheriff said, smiling.

Dixie *almost* said, "I don't have any elephants, but I have a coon," but she didn't. "I haven't gotten over to see Ollie and Patty yet."

"That's why I came by. It's Patty's birthday tomorrow, and she wanted me to invite you." Patty and Oliver were the sheriff's two children. They were about the same age as Dixie herself, and although she had disliked Ollie at one time, they had become good friends, too.

"Oh, that'll be fun, but I don't know if I can leave my aunt!"

"I'm sure Roy will be able to sit with her for a little while. The party's at two o'clock tomorrow afternoon. You be there for sure, Dixie!"

34

Dixie went to ask her aunt if she could go.

She received a favorable answer. "Why, I think you should. It can't be much fun staying around here taking care of an old woman."

"I don't mind, Aunt Edith. And you aren't an old woman." Dixie smiled and patted her hand. "I'll be sure to be back in time to fix supper."

When Dixie arrived at the sheriff's house, she found that the other guests were already there. Patty Peck, age ten, came running up and gave her a hard hug. "I'm so glad to see you, Dixie!" Patty had brown hair, brown eyes, and was a very pretty girl. She turned to say, "Look, Ollie, Dixie's here!"

Ollie was a miniature edition of his father. He came over right away, but, of course, he did not hug Dixie. It wouldn't be right for a boy to do such a thing! "Hi, Dixie," he said gruffly, but he couldn't conceal his pleasure.

"Hello, Ollie," Dixie said. "It's good to see you again. You've grown so much!"

Ollie shrugged. "Well, a fellow has to grow." He swallowed hard, then said, "You're looking . . . uh . . . real good."

Dixie smiled. She was wearing a short black skirt, a lime green top, and brown sandals. Her hair was fixed neatly, the way Aunt Sarah had taught her. She said, "Thank you, Ollie."

Then the other boys and girls began to crowd around. She was especially glad to see Leslie Stone, who had also been a good friend last summer. Leslie was there with her brother, Kelly. They were the children of Pastor James Stone from the local church, and both had his light hair and blue eyes.

Leslie was twelve, and Kelly was eleven, and the two seemed very glad to see her, especially Kelly.

There were games for some time. Then they listened to DC Talk, and afterward everybody went out to play badminton. At first they played singles, but then they chose sides, and this created a little difficulty.

Kelly Stone said, "You're my partner, aren't you, Dixie?"

Instantly Ollie Peck shoved his way between them. "No, she's not your partner! She's *my* partner!"

"Who died and made you king?" Kelly said. He grabbed Dixie's arm and pulled at her.

Ollie grabbed her other arm.

The two kept tugging at Dixie until Patty cried out, "Stop pulling at her! She's not the wishbone of a Christmas turkey!"

Ollie had very black eyes, and now they were flashing as he glared at Kelly Stone. "You always think you can do anything just because you're a preacher's kid!"

Kelly flushed. "And you always think you can do anything because you're a sheriff's kid!"

"Well, it's my sister's party, and I can pick anybody I please!"

"Wait! Wait a minute!" Dixie said. She was pleased that both boys wanted to have her for a partner, but things were getting a bit out of hand. "It doesn't matter who plays with who," she said quickly.

"Yes, it does!" Kelly said. "I chose you first, and you're my partner!"

Leslie took hold of her brother's arm, saying, "Kelly, be nice."

"I *am* nice, but Dixie's *my* partner!"

And then at that moment something happened that everybody soon regretted. To tell the truth, Ollie Peck was a little used to having his own way. And he knew his father was an important man in town. His face flushed with anger. He reached out and gave Kelly Stone a shove.

Kelly tripped over his own feet and sat down.

"Oh, don't do that!" Dixie cried. She turned to Kelly, who was getting up, and said, "Don't mind it, Kelly. Never mind."

But Kelly, without a word, threw himself at Ollie. The two boys went down, hitting each other and scuffling in the dirt. The other boys and girls formed a troubled circle around them, and Dixie tried her best to get them to stop, but they wouldn't.

"What's going on here?"

Suddenly Sheriff Peck was there. He reached down and grabbed the two boys, one in each hand, and yanked them apart by their belts. "What are you *doing,* Ollie?"

"It's his fault!" Ollie said.

"No, it isn't! It's his fault!" Kelly shot back. "I chose Dixie for a partner, and he started to fight!"

Sheriff Peck gave his son a hard look. "Ollie, is that true?"

"Well, it's my sister's party, and—"

"So it *is* true! All right, Kelly, since you asked Dixie first, she's your partner." He gave Ollie a hard look.

Ollie stared at Kelly, then at Dixie. "I didn't want to play badminton anyhow!" he said huffily, then stalked off.

Most of the fun had gone out of the party, at least for Dixie. She made it a point to look for Ollie later, though. He was sitting off by himself, looking rather forlorn. "I'm sorry about the fight," she said.

"If you're going to preach me a sermon, forget it! I'll get that from Dad later!"

Dixie hesitated. "Well, anyhow, I'm glad you wanted me for a partner."

Ollie suddenly looked up. "You are?"

"Why, sure! I thought about you and Patty a lot while I was gone with the circus."

He looked pleased. "Well—I thought about you, too."

"You know, it'd be a good thing if you and Kelly would apologize."

"Let *him* apologize!"

"But you too, Ollie. After all, you pushed him."

"Maybe I did, but he didn't have any business butting in."

Dixie saw there was little reasoning with him. She shrugged her shoulders. "Well, anyway, I think it's too bad it happened." She turned away and went to join the others.

When it was time to go home, Dixie noticed that Leslie Stone didn't say much. *I wonder what's wrong with her all of a sudden,* Dixie thought.

She found out the next day, when Patty came over to spend the afternoon. They enjoyed each other's company. They were playing Nintendo, when suddenly Patty said, "You better watch out for Leslie Stone, Dixie."

"Leslie? Why should I watch out for her? She's my friend." Dixie looked up from the game with a puzzled expression.

Patty laughed. "Oh, when Ollie asked you to be his partner at badminton instead of Leslie, I could see she was mad. She wanted Ollie to pick *her.*"

"Oh, it was just a silly game."

"Well, Leslie may be a preacher's kid, but she's used to having her own way. And now she sees that you're getting lots of attention." She grinned at Dixie and said, "Quite a homecoming you had. First party you go to, you cause a fight, and make the preacher's daughter mad, and get the sheriff's son in trouble."

Dixie glared at Patty indignantly. "I didn't mean to do any of those things!"

"I know it," Patty said. She patted Dixie's hand. "It looks like you're just one of those people that cause trouble wherever they go." She laughed then and said, "I didn't mean it. It's nice having you back, Dixie. It really is."

4
BARBIE DOLLS

The days on the farm passed quickly for Dixie. She had forgotten how much fun it was to be outside by herself.

Candy Sweet took her fishing several times, and they caught many sun perch from the large creek that wound around the Snyder property. Candy knew a lot about everything outdoors. It seemed he knew the name of every bird and every bush and could show her animal tracks everywhere. Once, when showing her a set of tracks, he asked in his slow way, "Do you know what these are, Dixie?"

Dixie bent over and stared at the tracks. "No, what are they?"

"That's a coon. Lots of them around here."

Dixie *almost* mentioned Bandit, but

just then a red-tailed hawk flew over, and when Candy pointed it out to her, she forgot about the coon.

One day she went swimming with the Pecks and the Stones. The swimming hole had been formed by some sort of strange action of the water, turning a place in the creek into a large pond twenty feet across and very deep. It was fun jumping in from the high bank and making like a cannonball. What had not been fun was that Ollie and Kelly were still mad at each other, and Leslie obviously didn't like the attention that Ollie paid to Dixie.

Dixie spent more and more time with Bandit. Her uncle and aunt always went to bed very early, sometimes even at eight o'clock. They were in the habit of getting up at dawn, and even though Aunt Edith could not work, she could not break her sleeping habits. They would leave Dixie to watch television, or to read, or to write in her diary. And every night after they went to bed, she would listen for the sound of Bandit's feet scrabbling on the porch.

One night, Dixie was writing a letter to Aunt Sarah when she heard the approach of the coon. She smiled, put down her pen, and went to the kitchen. There she collect-ed some things she had saved for Bandit's nighttime snack. Stepping outside, she smiled at the coon, who came waddling across the porch.

"You're early tonight, Bandit." She sat down on the steps, stretched out her legs, and, holding a bowl of grapes, began to feed them to him one at a time. She could never get over how clever he was with his hands. Most animals, she knew, had no thumbs, but Bandit did, and he could pick up a grape or any other small object and hold it as well as she herself could.

Finally the raccoon became impatient. He grabbed the edge of the bowl and tried to get it away from her.

"No, you can't have it!" she said. "You've got to learn better table manners!"

Bandit, like all coons, seemed to be smiling, but actually he was fussing at her, making a little clucking noise in his throat. He tugged at the bowl, and Dixie held onto it, laughing.

"No, I said! You can't have it! Now, just take one at a time."

Still holding onto the bowl, Bandit began to reach in and take his own grapes.

"You are so greedy!" Dixie scolded. "And you're getting so heavy!" He was a large animal. She had no way of knowing what he weighed.

He took another grape and stuffed it into his mouth.

After the grapes were gone, she said, "I brought you a present." Reaching into her pocket, she pulled out a package of M&M's. When she opened the package and placed a few on the porch floor, he picked up one of the small, hard candies and looked at it cautiously.

This time the raccoon hurried over to the bowl of water Dixie had set out for him. He began to wash the candy.

"Well, you do have neat manners after all!" Dixie smiled. She watched as he ate the M&M and returned to devour the rest.

"I wonder if there's anything you *won't* eat!" she said.

For a long time she sat watching the coon, who, after he had eaten, prowled around the porch. He definitely *waddled*. She said, "You sure are fat! I'll have to put you on a diet!"

Every night after that, Dixie brought out not only dog food and grapes but also

M&M's. She'd bought a goodly supply at the store, and every night she fed them to Bandit for dessert.

"I ought not to be doing this," she said. "You're fat as a butterball *now*." She could not resist him, however. He was so cute when he took up the tiny candies with his little hands and ate them delicately.

One Thursday morning Patty came over again, and the two girls spent the day together. Patty was a great collector of Barbie dolls, as was Dixie herself. Most of Dixie's she had left at the circus, but she had nine with her.

As they began playing with the dolls, Patty said, "Leslie thinks Barbie dolls are silly. She used to have one or two, but she says she never really liked Barbies."

"Why, at the circus there was a boy— Mickey Sullivan—even *he* liked Barbie dolls."

"What did he do? Was he one of the acrobats?"

"No, his father has an elephant act. The whole family's in it. I get to ride on one of their elephants in the parade at the beginning and ending of the show."

"Oh, I bet that's fun! How do you get on?"

Dixie began to tell her about life with the circus, and Patty listened, as the two continued to play with the dolls. Finally Patty said, "I didn't know boys *ever* liked to play with dolls."

"Some do. Mickey did. We'd give them all names, and we'd act out little games with them. He'd take the boy dolls, and I'd take the girl dolls, and they would go out to play tennis together. It was fun, and Mickey liked it."

"Didn't the other boys make fun of him?"

"Sometimes they did, but after a while Mickey didn't care. We were really best friends."

"I wish I could go live with the circus," Patty said, looking woeful. "I get tired of doing the same thing all the time. Get up, and eat, and go to school, and . . ."

"Well, the circus is a hard life. You move around all the time. And you have to live in a trailer. Everything has to be put away. When you have a room in a house," Dixie said, "if you leave something on the floor, it doesn't matter so much. But when you live in a small trailer like Aunt Sarah and I do, everything has to be put away all the time."

"I wouldn't care." Patty shook her head rebelliously. "Maybe Daddy will let me go back with you when your aunt gets well."

"I wish he would," Dixie said. "We could have a lot of fun together."

"One thing," Patty said suddenly, "you'd never get *Leslie* to go with you. She really doesn't like you anymore. She likes to get all the attention herself. She's so pretty and smart, but she's always been able to get her own way."

"I always thought Leslie was a sweet girl."

"Oh, she is!" Patty said. She was putting a dress on one of the Barbie dolls. It was a light blue sundress with a bright pink jacket. A white straw hat with pink-and-blue ribbons was perched on the doll's head. Patty held it up for Dixie's admiration. "Isn't that pretty?" Then she said, "Leslie's fine as long as she gets her own way and all the attention. But if she doesn't, look out! And you do get a lot of attention when you're here."

"I think you're making too much of it. Come on. Let's listen to some CDs."

They listened to Point of Grace, and Michael W. Smith, and some songs by Jaci

Velasquez, and they talked about the music. They both liked Christian music very much.

When it was time to put the dolls away, Patty suddenly said, "There's something maybe you ought to know, but I'm not sure it would be right for me to tell you."

Surprised, Dixie looked at her friend. "What is it, Patty? You can tell me."

"Well, Leslie's saying some things about you that aren't too nice."

Again Dixie was surprised. She had always liked Leslie when she had stayed on the farm the previous summer. "Then don't tell me what they are," she said. "I don't want to know."

"All right," Patty agreed. She looked at Dixie cautiously, then said, "She has her own little group of friends, and they do anything she says."

"Yes, I've always known that. She's a leader."

"Well, I just thought I'd tell you."

Dixie thought about what Patty had said as she fixed supper that night. It was macaroni and cheese, which was easy to prepare, but then she set out to make a chocolate pie. She had not had much success with her pies, and she worked especially hard on it. When she finally took the crust out of the oven, she was relieved to see that it looked just right. She poured in the filling, and spread the meringue on top, and was very pleased with it.

As usual, Candy ate with the family, and afterward he went out to sit on the porch. Candy ordinarily did not talk much, but he had had a great deal of experience hunting and fishing, and Dixie liked to hear his stories. Then it began to grow dark, and the skies were redder than Dixie had ever seen them.

Candy arose and said, "Better get to bed. Morning comes early."

"Candy, I need to talk to somebody."

Candy Sweet sat back down in the rocking chair. "What about?"

"It's about Leslie Stone."

"You mean the preacher's daughter?"

"Yes." Dixie hesitated, then leaned forward. "You must never tell anybody, Candy. This is just between us."

"I don't talk to many folks. I won't say nothing."

"Well, Leslie doesn't like me anymore. She's been saying some bad things about me to her friends. Especially the girls that she hangs out with."

"What's she saying?"

"I don't really know. Didn't ask."

"I reckon that's best."

Dixie waited for the big man to say more, but he did not. Finally she said, "What do you think I ought to do?"

Candy looked at her with surprise. "Do about what?" he asked, just as if she had not spoken.

Dixie was upset. "Do about Leslie saying bad things about me!"

"Why, that's her problem. It's not yours."

Dixie had become very upset over what Patty had told her, but she could not help smiling at Candy's response. "What do you mean by that?"

"Well, she's the one that's doing wrong. Not you. That's what I mean—it's her problem. Are you mad at her for saying those things?"

"Well, a little bit."

Candy shook his head. He ran his hand through his hair and thought for a moment. Then he said, "Well, it ain't what she says that matters most. It's the way you take it.

If you just go on and ignore it and don't get mad, then she hasn't hurt you. But if you begin to fuss and stew about it, and you get mad, then she has. I reckon it's up to you, Dixie." He rose from his chair, saying, "I'd say just don't think no more about it," and he lumbered off toward the bunkhouse.

Dixie sat on the porch for a long time thinking about what Candy had said and about Leslie. When Bandit came, she got his grapes and M&M's. He was ready for her, making a chirping noise in his throat, and as she fed him the goodies one by one, she said, "Sometimes I wish I was a coon and didn't have any more problems."

Bandit stared at her almost as if he understood. His little hands were so cute as he held the M&M and made his chirping noises.

Dixie laughed. "I guess you're telling me that Candy's right. And I guess he is. I just won't worry about Leslie and anything she says."

5

DIXIE LOSES HER TEMPER

The town council of Cedarville had been in session for three hours. Most of the men and women on the council were irritated and ready to drown the chairman, a tall man named Fred Smith. It was not only that Fred Smith had badly fitting dentures that almost fell out every time he got excited and tried to shout—which was often—but he was long-winded and hated to close a meeting.

Mrs. Mason, a short woman with gray hair and snapping blue eyes, said, "Mr. Chairman, I move that we adjourn!"

"Out of order, Ada!" Mr. Smith said. "We've got business!"

"Well, I've got business at home!" Ada said. "I have to cook. If I had nothing else to do but sit around talking, it wouldn't matter!"

Fred Smith's face grew red, and he began speaking so rapidly that his false teeth rattled. "I won't have that kind of remark in a meeting! We've got to keep our dignity!"

"I'm in favor of keeping our dignity," Sheriff Peck said, "but Ada's right. It is getting late."

Sheriff Peck was not a member of the council itself but had been invited for the purpose of enlightening them on the state of the police department in Cedarville. He was shifting back and forth in his chair and, glancing around, had noticed the impatience of everyone. "What more business can you have, Fred?" he asked. "It seems to me everything's been covered."

"Well, there's one thing that hasn't been covered," Mr. Smith said angrily, "and that's the business of these blasted coons!"

"Are we going to hear about that again?" Sheriff Peck groaned. "It comes up at every meeting."

"I know it does, but we're going to do something this time!"

Mrs. Mason shook her head. "My roast

is in the oven, and it's going to burn! This isn't a problem that we have to solve tonight!"

"Yes, it is, and we're going to stay here until I get a vote out of you!" Fred Smith said.

He began to talk, and fifteen minutes later he had laid out the problem. Everyone in town, according to his speech, was being invaded by coons coming in from the countryside. They were getting into garbage, getting under houses, and becoming a general nuisance.

Finally Mr. Smith said, "Why, right now I've got a whole pack of the pesky things under my house!"

"What do you expect to do about it?" George Swanson demanded. He was a heavyset man. He owned the Swanson Hardware store. "We can't afford to have a full-time animal control officer, and you know it, Fred."

"Well, we've got to do something, and I intend to stay here until we make a decision!"

Finally Mr. Smith made the motion himself. "I move that we hire a trapper to come in and get rid of these coons, and that we do it right now!"

The council was sick to death of the meeting and saw that there would be no getting around it. The motion was seconded and passed.

As Sheriff Peck left the room, he said to George Swanson, "Big doings for a few little pesky coons."

"Well, you know Fred. He's got to rule or ruin." George Swanson grinned at him. "Now we'll have to find a good man to get rid of the critters, I suppose."

The water of the big pond was almost as smooth as glass. The white clouds overhead were mirrored in its surface. The blue sky looked hard enough to strike a match on.

"What a day for fishing!" Ollie Peck was stretched out lazily, his hands locked behind his head. His eyes were barely open as he watched his red-and-white cork being blown by the slight breeze that gently ruffled the water now and then.

Dixie, sitting on a tree stump a few feet away, held her pole in both hands. She looked with disgust at Ollie and exclaimed, "You're not going to catch any fish like that!"

"I bet I catch more than you do. I've already got four, and you only got two."

Dixie sniffed but could not argue, for that was true enough.

She and Ollie had come down to this pond on the south side of the Snyder property an hour earlier. They had spent most of the time throwing rocks at the turtles that kept poking their heads up. They had brought fishing lines, however, and Dixie insisted that they try to catch enough fish for supper.

"I'm going over there and see if there's not a big bass around those lilies out there," she said.

"Ah, that's too much work. Let the bass come over here."

Dixie stared at him, then laughed. "You're the laziest fisherman I ever saw!"

"Fellow's got to use his head," Ollie muttered. The sun was warm, and he looked sleepy. But then he suddenly sat up and shook his shoulders. "Well, maybe you're right. We're not getting any bites here. Come on." He grinned and said, "There's probably more fish over in those lily pads. I'm glad I thought of it."

Dixie glared at him but jerked up her pole and bait can.

The two made their way around to the far side of the pond, where the water was much deeper. They threw their lines out.

Almost at once Dixie's cork disappeared with a *plop!* Her pole bent double, and she hauled back on it, crying excitedly, "I've got a monster, Ollie!"

"Give him some slack! You're going to break the line!"

"I guess I know how to fish!" she shouted back. But it was, in truth, the biggest fish she had ever caught, and for a while it seemed she could not get him in.

Then the fish broke the water, and Ollie shouted, "It's a *bass!* A big one! Hang onto him, Dixie!"

Dixie kept the pole arched, and finally the fish tired.

"Bring him in, and I'll get him!" Ollie cried. He waded out knee-deep into the pond and, as Dixie walked backward, waited until the fish was near. Then, reaching down, he grabbed him with his thumb inside the open mouth and hauled him up. "Look at him! What a beauty!" he said, and he brought the flopping fish to shore.

Dixie stared at her fish. Her heart was beating fast, and she said, "That's the biggest fish I ever caught!"

"You ought to have this one mounted," Ollie said.

Dixie thought about it. "No, we don't have enough for supper with just the little ones."

"Yeah, but if you mount this one, you can look at him forever. Put him right up over the fireplace."

They argued about whether to eat the fish or have it mounted, but Dixie finally prevailed. "Come on. Let's go home and show it to everybody."

They quickly gathered their bait, poles, and stringer of fish and returned to the house. Dixie carried the fish up to the front porch, where Uncle Roy was sitting, whittling on a piece of cedar. "Look what I caught," she said proudly.

"My, that *is* a fine fish! Did you get that out of the pond? Didn't know there was any that big in there."

"Well, this one's not there anymore. I'm going to show it to Aunt Edith." Dixie walked inside, carrying the fish right into the living room.

Her aunt, sitting in her wheelchair, exclaimed, "Get that fish out of here!"

"Aw, Aunt Edith, I wanted you to see it!"

Aunt Edith relented. "Well, it *is* a fine fish. Did you catch it yourself?"

"I sure did. Isn't he pretty?"

"Well, I expect we'll have fish for supper tonight."

Dixie grinned and nodded. "We sure will. I'm going to clean him right now."

She went out the back door and around front, where Ollie was explaining why Dixie caught the big fish instead of him. "I would have caught that fish myself. I knew there was a big one in there, but I decided to let Dixie catch it. So I let her put her line in first."

Dixie grinned at him. "Thanks a lot, Ollie. Just for that you can help me clean the fish."

They went around to the backyard, where they unstrung all the smaller fish. Dixie said, "I've never cleaned a fish as big as this bass. Let's get the brim clean first, then we'll worry about him."

They cleaned the smaller fish quickly. "I can cook these whole," she said. "They're not too big."

"What about this bass?"

"I don't know. He's too big to serve whole." She looked up then and saw Candy Sweet. "Candy, do you know how to clean a big fish?"

Candy Sweet was walking across the yard, a shovel over his shoulder. He came over and looked down at the bass and smiled. "Big fish."

Silently, he reached out and took the long butcher knife from Dixie. Then he grabbed the fish by the mouth. He cut a slice right below the head, then slowly ran the knife down the fish's ribs. When he got to the tail, he flipped the whole thing over. When he was through cutting, he said, "That's half of it."

Then he cut off the other side of the fish and held it up. "This is called a fillet," he said. "No bones at all."

"Oh, Candy, that's enough to feed us all, along with the little ones!"

"Good. I like fish." And Candy walked away.

As Dixie and Ollie were washing their hands under the faucet in the yard, Ollie said, "Did you hear what they decided to do about the coons?"

"What who decided to do?"

"The town council. My dad was there. He told me about it."

"What did they decide to do?"

"They decided to trap all the coons in town. They're gonna hire somebody to do it. I'd like to have that job!"

Dixie stopped washing her hands and stared at Ollie with large eyes. "What will they do with them?"

"Oh, kill 'em, I guess. They're good to eat, you know. Lots of people eat coon."

"How awful!"

"Awful? What's awful about it? You eat squirrels and venison and . . ."

"But coons are different. They're so— so cute."

Ollie swung the towel and popped at Dixie with it. "So are calves cute, but we eat *them.*"

Ollie went home soon after that, but all the while Dixie was cooking supper she was thinking about what he had said.

She knew how to fry fish, and she fried potatoes to go with them. And she made hush puppies. It was one of her favorite meals, and she had learned to do it well.

After the blessing, Candy took one bite of fish and said, "Boy, this is *good!*"

Everyone agreed, and all of the fish soon disappeared.

Candy helped Dixie wash the dishes, and she told him what Ollie had said about the raccoons.

"Don't see that the coons are hurtin' anybody, but that's how people are."

Dixie kept thinking about the coons. That night when she went out to feed Bandit, she said, "Bandit, we're going to have to do something. I can't let that animal man get you."

Bandit looked at her, gurgled in his throat, and asked for more grapes.

That night Dixie had nightmares about someone chasing Bandit and putting him in a cage and hauling him off.

For two days she worried about the raccoons.

On Sunday morning Dixie went to church. She was wearing a light green dress that had short sleeves and a scoop neckline and was buttoned up the front with small white buttons in the shape of hearts.

When she saw the Pecks sitting up

near the front, she whispered to her uncle, "I'm going up and sit with Ollie and Patty."

She started down the aisle. Then, just as she started to slide in and sit down, somebody bumped into her. The bump knocked her off balance, and she turned to see Leslie Stone standing there, wearing a dress even prettier than Dixie's.

Leslie did not even apologize. Instead, she slid into the seat beside Ollie. She looked up at Dixie and smiled, whispering, "You can sit on the end, Dixie."

The service began then, but that service did Dixie little good. She was furiously angry at Leslie and hardly heard a word that Pastor Stone said. She even found herself thinking of ways to get even.

When the service was over and she got up to leave the building, Dixie felt a hand on her arm and turned around to see Kelly, Leslie's brother, behind her.

"I saw what Leslie did. Bumping into you and pushing you out of the way."

Dixie said, "She was so mean!"

"She gets like that sometimes," Kelly said. "She's used to having her own way."

"She didn't have to push me like that.

She could have just asked me—I would have let her sit beside Ollie!"

He grinned then. "Next time, you come over and sit by me."

Dixie ordinarily would have smiled and said, "Sure, I will," but she was still angry. She left the church, and all the way home she was thinking about Leslie Stone. "I don't care if she *is* prettier than I am—and the preacher's daughter! She shouldn't have done that!"

Off and on all day long, she thought about the incident, and that night she told Bandit about it. She had grown accustomed to talking to the big coon, just as if he knew what she was saying. She wound up by saying, "I'm so mad at her I could spit! And I didn't get a thing out of church!"

Bandit began to eat M&M's.

"All right. Here, take them all." Dixie watched as the raccoon ate the candies. Then she said, "I'm going to get even with her! You see if I don't!"

6
A BAD GUY

For the next few days Dixie was very protective of Bandit. She kept waiting to hear about the city council's hiring someone to eliminate all the coons in town, and at night she would even pray for Bandit and all the other coons.

Sometimes she wondered if it was right to pray for coons. Finally she said, "Lord, I know You care about sparrows, and if You care about sparrows, You must love the coons too."

Next Friday she went to a sleepover at Patty's and was somewhat upset to find that Patty had invited Leslie Stone. She tried to put her problem out of her mind, though, for she knew that it was wrong to hold grudges and to have hard feelings.

The three sat around and watched *The*

Lion King, for the video had been one of Patty's birthday presents. They all liked that movie very much, and Patty sighed when it was over, saying, "I could watch that every night, I think."

Leslie shrugged her shoulders. They were all three wearing pajamas, and Leslie's were a pale pink. She said, "I like more grown-up movies. Cartoons are all right, but I'm pretty tired of them."

Dixie looked at Leslie and wondered if that was really true. She had noticed that Leslie always seemed to enjoy any cartoon-type movies that they saw and was always anxious for the next Walt Disney. She said, "Well, I like all kinds of good movies."

Patty insisted on playing with the Barbie dolls for a while, but soon Leslie grew impatient. She did not like to play with dolls, she said, as she often did. "This is for little kids. Let's play Monopoly."

The girls soon were seated on the floor, moving their game pieces around and changing money. Leslie was very good at Monopoly and almost always won. *That's probably the reason she likes to play it so much,* Dixie thought.

When Leslie did win the game, she

smiled with contentment and said, "I think I'm just naturally good at this game. Maybe I'll be a millionaire when I grow up. Then I can sell real houses and hotels."

Neither Dixie nor Patty, apparently, was interested in being rich.

Patty stood up and said, "Well, I guess we'd better brush our teeth and go to bed. Mom will get us up at the crack of dawn, as usual."

Dixie knew that Sheriff Peck was in on all the business at city hall, and she decided to ask Patty the question that had been in her mind all evening. "Patty, has your dad said any more about the coons?"

"I don't think so. They're looking for someone to get rid of them."

"I wish they wouldn't do that." Dixie frowned.

She went into the bathroom with the other girls, where they all put Pepsodent on their toothbrushes and began brushing hard. With her mouth full of foam, Dixie said, "I don't think it's right to get rid of animals like that."

"What's wrong with it?" Leslie demanded. "They're pests!"

"They don't cause that much trouble,"

Dixie argued. She rinsed her mouth, and the other two did the same.

Then they all went back and climbed into the big bed that they were sharing. Leslie and Dixie were on the outside, and Patty was in the middle.

"They *are* pests! They get into garbage cans and gardens, and Dad said that when coons get big they can even kill small pets like kittens and dogs."

"I never heard of anything like that!" Dixie said, frowning again.

The discussion went on for some time, and the more Dixie argued for the coons, the more Leslie seemed in favor of getting rid of them. Finally she said, "They all ought to be shot! They're not any good for anything!"

Then Dixie did grow angry. She knew she should keep her thoughts to herself, but she said, "Birds aren't any 'good' for anything, either! Would you be in favor of going around and shooting all the robins and bluebirds?"

"That's different!" Leslie said. "They don't get into the garbage cans. And they *sing.*"

Patty disliked arguments. "Let's not

argue about it," she said. "I'm sleepy. Good night."

"Good night," Dixie said, but she lay awake for a long time, struggling with her feelings about Leslie. *She's so mean,* she thought. *Anybody that would kill a cute animal like Bandit has to be mean!*

She tried to say her prayers but didn't have a great deal of success. Finally she sighed and thought, *Lord, You know I'm mad at Leslie, and You know I'm worried about the coons. My prayers aren't real good at the moment.*

The next day, which was Saturday, Dixie got a rude shock. She went with Patty downtown, where they stopped by the jail to visit Patty's dad. Dixie always liked to do that, for Sheriff Peck nearly always took them out for banana splits at the TCBY. He sat there and ate one with them today.

After they finished their ice cream, he started back to the jail, one girl on either side of him. They were about to go past the fire station when he said, "Uh-oh! Looks like Neil Sparks has been busy!"

"Who's Neil Sparks, Daddy?" Patty asked.

"Why, he's the fellow they hired to rid the town of coons. That's him over there. Looks like he's already made a haul."

Dixie stared at the skinny man wearing blue jeans, a dirty T-shirt, and a ball cap on backwards. As they drew closer, she saw that he was grinning widely as he talked with two of the firemen. He was saying, "Yeah, it takes a real trapper to get this job done. Look at what I got in just one night!"

Dixie stopped abruptly, for there in two cages were several raccoons. They were rearing up against the sides of the cages. Their little paws were gripping the wire, and their noses were wiggling.

Sheriff Peck said, "Howdy, fellas. Hello, Neil."

"Why, howdy, Sheriff. Look here at what I got. Seven coons just last night. Why, it won't take me no time to get all these coons out of here for you."

Dixie went over to the cage and started to put her fingers through the wire. The coons immediately crowded toward her.

"Hey, little girl, get away from them coons! You're liable to get bit!"

"They're not going to bite me! Look how tame they are!" Dixie protested.

74

"You never know. You don't know coons like I do! Why, a big boar coon, he can kill a dog, and besides they might have rabies!"

"He's right, Dixie," the sheriff said.

Dixie felt sorry for the coons and wished she could turn them loose. She also felt like keeping her fingers against the cage, but she didn't.

Patty came over and stood beside her. She did not put her fingers near the wire, for she was afraid of animals except for kittens and small dogs. She looked at Dixie's face and asked, "What's the matter, Dixie?"

"I feel sorry for the coons. I hate to see anything caged up."

"Well, they won't be caged long." Neil Sparks grinned. He laughed as if he had said something funny, then winked at the firemen. "We'll take care of these little varmints!"

"Come along, Dixie," Sheriff Peck said. "I've got to get you home."

Dixie looked at the coons for just one moment more, then turned away. She felt so bad she wanted to cry, and she knew that both Patty and the sheriff could see she was unhappy.

"I was against all this," Sheriff Peck said, "but Fred Smith, he gets an idea in his head and nothing else will do."

Dixie said very little as Sheriff Peck and Patty drove her home. When she got out of the car, she said, "Thanks for inviting me to the sleepover. It was fun."

"We'll do it again soon," Patty said. She hesitated, then reached over and patted Dixie's hand. "Don't worry. It'll be all right."

"No, it won't!" Dixie said shortly.

She turned and walked toward the house, then saw Candy Sweet cutting the grass. She stood and watched him for a while.

Soon Candy stopped the mower and came over to her. "Well, did you have a good time at your friend's house?"

"It was OK—but, Candy, they've got a man in town that's trapping the coons! His name is Neil Sparks."

"Neil Sparks!" He frowned and shook his head but said nothing else.

"Do you know him?" Dixie asked.

"Yeah, I knows him all right. He's one of those Sparks kids from over in Pine Bluff."

"I didn't like him. He was laughing because he had trapped the coons. He had

76

seven of them, and—oh, Candy, they looked so pitiful in those cages!"

Candy Sweet seemed at a loss for words. He probably wanted to comfort Dixie and didn't know what to say. "Well, maybe it will be all right," he mumbled.

But Dixie heard something in his voice that troubled her. "What will he do with them—the coons?"

Candy was a simple man, and he told the simple truth. "I expect he'll sell their fur and then sell the meat."

It was what Dixie was afraid of. She looked up at Candy, and tears formed in her eyes. All she could think of was the pitiful little coons, and two of them had been little more than babies. She began to walk slowly away, saying nothing more as Candy turned and went back to the lawn mower, started it up, and began cutting grass again.

7
THE MASTER PLAN

The whole town was soon talking about how well Neil Sparks was doing catching raccoons. Dixie didn't want to hear any of it, for it made her sad. Whenever coons were mentioned, she would turn around and walk away.

By the time three days had passed, she had figured out that sooner or later Neil Sparks would come to the Snyder place, set his traps, and poor Bandit wouldn't have any better sense than to walk right into one. *He's so trusting,* she thought. *If he sees something good to eat in a trap, he'll go right in. And then Neil Sparks will have him, and he'll kill him.*

The end of May came, and Dixie was still thinking of little else other than the raccoons. She wrote letters to Aunt Sarah and to her parents in Africa, but she didn't mention the coons to either of them.

If Aunt Sarah were here, or if Mama and Daddy were here, she thought, *I could tell them, and I bet one of them would do something about it.* She had no idea what, but she had great confidence in her aunt and in her parents. But she didn't want to worry her uncle and aunt with the problem. There was nothing they could do about it anyway.

On the last day of the month, she was sitting on the porch late one afternoon with Uncle Roy and Aunt Edith. The sun was going down, and they were watching the swallows as they swooped and rolled like acrobats in the air over by the barn.

"Who's that?" Uncle Roy said, squinting.

"Don't know that truck," Aunt Edith said.

Dixie knew it, though. "That's Neil Sparks," she said and gritted her teeth, for she knew what was coming.

The pickup stopped, and Neil Sparks got out. He was wearing the same dirty T-shirt and was chewing tobacco today. He stopped before the three sitting on the porch and said, "Howdy, folks. Just came by to tell you I'll be headin' this way in a couple of days. My name's Neil Sparks. I'm the trapper."

"Oh, you're the man they hired to get rid of the coons!" Uncle Roy said.

"That's me!" Sparks said, nodding happily. "And I'm gettin' the job done, too!" He stood bragging about what a great job he was doing, then winked at Dixie. "Don't you worry about them coons bein' around, missy. I'll take care of every one of them. See you probably day after tomorrow."

Dixie watched as Neil Sparks sauntered back to his truck, got in, and started it up again. She looked at her uncle and aunt and almost said something but again realized there was nothing they could do. *I've got to do something,* she thought, *but I don't know what.*

For the rest of the afternoon and until her uncle and aunt went to bed, she had the problem of Bandit on her mind. After Uncle Roy and Aunt Edith went to bed, she went to her own room and sat down in the middle of the bed. "There's got to be something I can do," she said out loud.

Finally she got Bandit's food and went out onto the porch. Because of the danger, perhaps, he seemed cuter and dearer to her than ever. He had gotten to the point where he would come very close and touch her hand with his little paw. He was so gentle, and he looked so cute with his black mask and his black, shiny eyes that Dixie wanted to pick him up and hug him.

"I can't let anything happen to you, Bandit! I just can't!"

Bandit made the gurgling noise in his throat.

Dixie went inside and, since they were out of grapes, brought out a box of raisins. He seemed to like those just as well. He would take the tiny raisins in his hands and chew them up. It took a great deal of chewing, but finally he finished most of the box.

"That's all for tonight, Bandit," she whispered, getting up.

He gurgled at her.

Then Dixie said, "Wait a minute!" Bandit looked at her, and she said, "I've got an idea." She held out a raisin. "Come on, Bandit." She walked to the front door and opened it. "Come on, I'm going to try something," she said. "Come. Here's a raisin."

Bandit looked at her with his bright eyes and then entered the house. He was very curious and sniffed around at the floor and at some of the furniture, but Dixie whispered, "Come on. I've got something real good for you."

She went to the refrigerator, took out an apple, and cut it into small chunks. He watched her, and she gave him a piece, which he at once ate.

Dixie whispered, "Now, you be quiet! I'll get you some water." Carefully she got down a deep bowl, filled it with water, then said, "Come on, Bandit. I've got a place for you where that old Neil Sparks can't get you."

A door opening off the hall went down into the cellar. Dixie switched on the light and said, "Come on, Bandit." Holding a piece of apple toward the coon, she went down the stairs, and Bandit followed her.

He was a little cautious at first, but when they got downstairs, he began to look around. The cellar was not used for anything but storage. It was full of wooden crates and some old fishing gear. The walls were lined with shelves where Aunt Edith kept her glass jars for canning.

Dixie found a piece of blanket and put it on the dirt floor, saying, "Here's a good bed for you, and I'll leave the rest of this apple. You be quiet now, and I'll come and let you out before Uncle Roy and Aunt Edith get up."

Bandit seemed perfectly happy. He sat there eating the apple, and then Dixie stroked his fur, saying, "You be quiet and don't wake anybody up."

She waited until Bandit made his gurgling noise and then left the cellar.

Dixie went to her bedroom, undressed and brushed her teeth, then got into bed, beginning to wonder if she had done the right thing. "I'll have to get up real early in the morning so that Aunt Edith and Uncle Roy won't hear him."

She set her clock alarm, and when it went off early the next morning, she quickly shut it off. It was the tiny alarm clock that her mother had given her before they left for Africa. It made a tiny, silvery sound, and Dixie waited to see if anyone else had heard it. There was no noise, however, and she got up and went to the cellar right away.

She found Bandit, who greeted her at once, and with a bread crust she led him up through the house and outside. It was still dark, and he disappeared at once.

Dixie drew a sigh of relief. "Well, I know what to do about Bandit from now on. When that old Neil Sparks sets his traps, he'll just see how many coons he gets from around here!"

Dixie's plan seemed to work very well. For the next two nights, she let Bandit into the house and put him in the cellar after her uncle and aunt had gone to bed. Then she got up early and let him out. On the third day, however, something went wrong. Evidently she hadn't closed tightly the door that led to the cellar, for when she went to get Bandit she saw it was standing open.

Going down the stairs, she called for him, "Bandit, come on!" But no Bandit! Quickly she searched the cellar, then her heart gave a jump.

"He's gotten loose!" she cried. She went upstairs in a panic but found him almost at once. He was just coming out of the kitchen. She ran over to him and said, "Bandit, what have you been into? Never mind. It's time to go outside." He seemed reluctant to go out, and finally she had to pick him up and carry him out. "Go on, now. I'll see you tonight."

She went into the kitchen and found that he had gotten into some of the lower cabinets. Fortunately, the only thing he'd really done damage to was the potatoes. He had obviously eaten several of them. Dixie shoved the others back into the cabinet, shut the door, and drew a deep sigh of relief. *I'll have to shut that cellar door more carefully,* she thought.

After breakfast, Uncle Roy went into the living room to read his paper as he usually did. Dixie was washing the dishes when he came back, a puzzled frown on his face. "I can't figure this out, Dixie. Come and look at it."

"What is it, Uncle Roy?" Dixie asked.

"Come on and see."

Dixie followed him into the living room, and he pointed to something beside his chair. "Look at that," he said.

Dixie looked closer and saw that it was the silvery wrappings that covered Hershey's chocolate kisses.

"You dropped your papers on the floor," she said.

Uncle Roy, who loved Hershey's Kisses, shook his head. "I never do that. I always stick them in my pocket." He looked at

Dixie and said, "Did you eat some after we went to bed?"

And Dixie knew instantly what had happened. *Bandit* had eaten them! Taking them out of their wrappings would be no problem for him with his clever little hands.

She did not want to lie to her uncle, so she did not answer either way. "I'm sorry, Uncle Roy."

"Well, you're welcome to the candy, but I just thought it's not like you to make a mess like that," he said. He sat down and began reading the paper.

Dixie quickly began to pick up the wrappers. Now she felt bad, for she knew she had misled her uncle. She tried to persuade herself that it was all right, thinking, *I didn't tell him that I ate them. He just assumed that.* Still, she knew it wasn't right. She thought about telling him the truth. Then she thought, *Well, Neil Sparks won't stay around here forever. He'll have to go away sometime. Then I'll tell Uncle Roy.*

That night she didn't know what to do to keep Bandit in, for the lock on the door was broken.

"So that's how you got out." The door would close, but when anyone touched it from the inside it simply swung open again. "I can get Uncle Roy to fix the door, but what am I going to do with you until he does?" Finally she said, "You can stay in my room tonight, that's what."

Bandit did not seem to mind staying in her bedroom. He went around and smelled everything, and Dixie had a fine time playing with him. She had brought up a lot of food, and he ate until his stomach bulged. At last she said, "Now, you can go to sleep, and when the alarm goes off you can go out."

Bandit curled into a ball and went to sleep on the rug beside Dixie's bed. Dixie reached down and petted him, then got into bed and said, "Well, you won't get into any mischief tonight." Then she went to sleep.

When the little silver bell went off the next morning, she awoke at once and shut it off. She looked over the side of the bed to speak to Bandit—but he was not there.

Coming out of bed in a flash, Dixie whispered, "Bandit, where are you?"

She heard a slight noise in the bathroom then. As soon as she stepped inside the bathroom, she whispered, *"Bandit, what have you done?"*

Bandit was sitting up in the lavatory. He had opened the medicine cabinet and taken everything out. This was where Dixie kept her toothpaste and vitamins and the makeup that she played with. It was all in there.

The floor was littered. Bandit had gotten the top off the powder and scattered it everywhere. His little footprints were in it. He had also gotten the top off the lipstick that had belonged to Aunt Sarah, which Dixie used just for play times. Somehow he had marked up the floor with that. Even now he had some on his mouth.

The room was an absolute mess! Every bottle, every jar, every can that could be opened had been opened and was scattered on the floor.

Dixie said, "Bandit, look what you've done! Aren't you ashamed?"

Bandit, however, was not ashamed. He sat and seemed to be smiling at her, and he gurgled in his throat. Dixie went over and scolded him. "Bandit, come on! You're going outside!"

Once she had coaxed Bandit outside, Dixie went back and began to clean up the mess.

I'll never do this again, she thought. *Who would have thought he could have gotten up here and opened this cabinet? I see why some people think raccoons are pests!*

She managed to get the bathroom cleaned up just in time to go down and cook breakfast.

At the breakfast table, Uncle Roy grinned at her. "You didn't eat any more of my Hershey's Kisses, did you?"

"No, I didn't, Uncle Roy."

"That's good. If you eat too many of them, you'll be fat and pretty like me," he said, teasing her as he always did.

"I thought I heard something in your room last night. Were you up late?" Aunt Edith asked. Then she added, "No, it couldn't have been that. It was in the middle of the night or early this morning."

Dixie knew she must have heard Bandit spilling some of the bottles in the bathroom. She had slept like a log herself and heard nothing. She said, "Maybe I got up to get a drink of water."

But after breakfast, as Dixie washed the dishes, she thought, *I'm being a liar. Why don't I just tell them the truth? I will —just as soon as Neil Sparks is gone.*

8
A STARTLING DEVELOPMENT

Two days after Bandit had gotten into Dixie's medicine cabinet, Neil Sparks arrived at the farm. He stopped off just at dusk and hauled a wire trap out of his truck.

Uncle Roy went out to meet him, shaking his head. "We ain't had no trouble with coons around here, Neil."

"You can't tell about coons." Sparks nodded confidently. He spit tobacco juice onto Aunt Edith's chrysanthemums and said, "I'll get 'em, you can bet on that! They'll come out of the woodwork sometime."

Dixie stood on the porch and watched as Neil Sparks set the trap and put a chunk of bread inside. "I just use stale bread. They eat anything, those coons will. I'll come by tomorrow and pick up what I catch."

After the truck pulled out, Uncle Roy said, "I don't like that fella. Them Sparkses never were any good. His brother's in the penitentiary for holdin' up a gas station. I reckon they just haven't caught this one yet."

Dixie still had said nothing to her uncle and aunt about Bandit. She felt bad about keeping secrets from them, but she consoled herself by thinking, *It'll soon be over. Then I won't have to put Bandit in the cellar anymore. And that old Neil Sparks will move on to somewhere else.*

By accident, Dixie found out that Bandit slept in the barn in the daytime. She startled him and herself one afternoon when she went in to find a rake to use in the garden. She heard a noise and found him bedded down on some old feed sacks.

"So this is where you sleep in the daytime." She grinned. "Well, that's good. Hardly anybody ever comes out here."

It became kind of a game to her, and she delighted in outwitting Neil Sparks. Uncle Roy repaired the cellar door lock, and every evening she would put Bandit in the cellar with plenty of food. In the morning when she let him out, she would spring Sparks's coon trap with a stick.

When Neil Sparks came by, he would look at the trap and shake his head.

Dixie would stand beside him and say, "I guess something sprung your trap, didn't it?"

"They're smart, some of these coons, but I never seen one do that." Sparks scratched his head and gritted his teeth. "I'll get him, though. You can be sure of it."

This went on for four or five days. Finally Neil Sparks said, "Well, I don't know what it is. Maybe it's a wildcat or something. One of those wildcats that roam the woods sometimes. Anyhow, it's plain there ain't no coons around here."

Dixie was delighted when he put the trap in his truck and drove off, an angry scowl on his face.

"Now you don't have to sleep in the cellar," she told Bandit, and that night she did not put him inside.

The next night when she set out to feed him she was surprised that he didn't come. She was waiting for him to come from the barn, and, when he didn't, she finally went out to look for him. He was not there, however, and she was a little afraid that he'd gone off to one of the neighbors' houses and gotten into a trap that Sparks had set there.

Dixie sat down on the porch steps. Then all of a sudden she heard a sound. Walking over to the side of the porch, she looked around and saw that the door that led to the *outside* cellar was pushed up a little, and Bandit was climbing out. It was an odd kind of door, lying flat with the ground, but Bandit had squeezed it open.

"What are you doing? You found your own door, didn't you?"

Bandit seemed pleased with himself. He began pawing at her shoes.

She bent over to pet him. "So, you like it in that root cellar, do you? Well, I guess you can stay there. Nobody *ever* goes down there, anyhow."

She fed the raccoon, and that night when she went to bed, she prayed, "Thank You, Lord, for taking care of Bandit and not letting Neil Sparks get him. And I do feel bad that I didn't tell the whole truth to Aunt Edith and Uncle Roy. I'm sorry. I knew better. I'll tell them, and I won't make up any half stories."

But Dixie *didn't* tell them. Not right away.

Dixie found life simpler now that Neil Sparks was not around the place with his traps. She went to church, she had a good time with the Cedarville boys and girls at the church affairs, and every night Bandit would come back.

The middle of June came, and she got to go to the baseball games and watch Ollie Peck and Kelly Stone, who both played on the team. She cheered for both of them equally. She tried to make better friends with Leslie Stone. But Leslie was still not very friendly.

She talked to Patty about it, who said, "There's not much you can do about Leslie. She's stubborn. She does what she wants to do, and that's all there is to it."

It was at the exact middle of the month, the fifteenth, that Dixie got one of the biggest shocks of her life. Her uncle and aunt had gone to bed, and, as usual, she had gotten the grapes and the M&M's and other food ready for Bandit.

She was sitting on the front porch, waiting for him to come out of the root cellar. She finally heard a tiny noise and turned to the steps as the raccoon appeared.

"There you are, Bandit. I guess you're starved to death as usual." Dixie got a grape ready, but suddenly another tiny sound caught her ear. She looked down at the steps and thought at first that she was seeing a rat. She gave a little squeal, for she did not like rats. She stood up to find a stick to throw at him, and then in the moonlight she saw that it was not a rat! What she saw was a baby raccoon.

"What in the world!" Dixie whispered. Even as she did, another little raccoon appeared—and then another, and then another. By the time Dixie got to the edge of the porch, she saw five baby raccoons at the steps.

Dixie could not believe her eyes. She looked at Bandit, and then the truth came to her. "You're not a *he!* You're a *she,* and these are your babies!"

Bandit seemed to be pleased. She nuzzled the baby raccoons, and they crowded around her.

Dixie went to the edge of the porch and sat down on the steps. The babies ran off at once, but she sat there quietly, and after a while they came back again, very shyly. She held out a grape and said, "Come on, you can have something to eat, too."

Bandit nudged herself closer to get the grape, but Dixie said, "No, these are for your babies."

It took Dixie some time to get the baby coons to take the grapes, and only two finally did come. She fed them and was delighted with how they ate hungrily.

Finally Bandit herded her cubs together by the outside cellar door and began to wash them just as a mother cat will wash her kittens.

Then the cubs began to play. They were very clumsy, and Dixie laughed to see them rolling and tumbling. They were so awkward they could not stay on their feet very well.

At last Bandit and her little flock all disappeared back down into the root cellar.

Dixie sat on the steps for a long time, thinking a lot about this new problem. *What am I going to do with five baby raccoons?* she wondered. Finally she shrugged her shoulders. "Well, I guess I'll find a way."

She finally did find a way, but for the next two weeks Dixie was thinking of little but coons. By the end of that time the babies were eating a lot, and Dixie had to go to the grocery store and buy more dog food.

Mr. Simms, the grocer, said, "How many dogs have you got, Dixie? You sure buy a lot of dog food."

Dixie could not think of an answer. She just said, "Thank you, Mr. Simms."

That night she tried desperately to think of a way to tell her uncle and aunt about Bandit and Bandit's babies, but nothing came to her.

The next day as she and Candy Sweet were working in the garden, the hired man suddenly said, "How are the baby coons getting along?"

Dixie stopped and stared at him. "You know about them?"

"Why, sure!" Candy seemed surprised. "I've seen them out a couple of nights. And besides, their tracks are all over the place."

"Do you think Uncle Roy knows about them?"

"I don't know. He's a little nearsighted. Maybe he didn't notice the tracks."

Dixie decided it was time to tell *somebody* the truth. "I've been hiding their mama, Candy. I didn't want Neil Sparks to get her."

"Well, he's still trapping some. Guess there was a lot of coons in this town. But he's not been around here lately."

"Candy, how am I going to feed all those coons and keep them a secret? He'll come for sure, if he hears about it." Dixie frowned. "I promised God I would tell the whole story to Uncle Roy and Aunt Edith, too, and I haven't. It's not right to keep secrets like that."

Candy seemed unable to think of anything to say to this. He pulled off his straw hat and scratched his head. "Well, I'll help you all I can, Dixie. Tell you what—as soon as they get big enough, I'll just take them off myself into the deep woods by the river bottom. They'll be all right there."

"Would you, Candy?" Dixie smiled then. She came over and grabbed his sleeve. "Will you help me with them?"

"Well," Candy Sweet grinned, looking down at her, "I helped you hide an elephant, so I guess gettin' rid of a few coons won't be much of a job."

"I'm glad I have a friend like you, Candy," Dixie said. She felt better and went to sleep more easily that night. She dreamed of raccoons, though, not just five but hundreds of coons. She saw their little ringed tails all over the place. But it was not a scary dream, and she felt, as she woke up the next morning, that somehow all would be well.

9

COON TROUBLE

"That dog of yours must eat a heap of dog food, Dixie!"

It was a beautiful Saturday afternoon. Mr. Simms, the grocery store owner in Cedarville, had just carried the groceries that Dixie had bought out to the pickup. Uncle Roy was getting a haircut, and she had bought the supplies.

Mr. Simms lifted the two large sacks of dry dog food into the back and leaned them against the cab. Shaking his head, he said, "What kind of dog have you *got*, a Saint Bernard?"

"No, Shep's just a Border collie."

"Well, he must eat a lot—as much dog food as you're buying."

Dixie said nothing more, for her conscience was troubling her. She still had never felt brave enough to tell her uncle and aunt about Bandit and the babies, and now they were half-grown! She thought about what she had said to Mr. Simms and comforted herself by thinking, *Well, it wasn't a real lie. Shep does eat a lot—for a Border collie.*

She climbed into the front seat of the pickup to wait for Uncle Roy. She slipped a CD into the player and clipped the earphones over her head. Turning up the volume, she began to listen to one of her favorite Michael W. Smith songs. She sang along with him and was so engrossed in the music that she was startled when suddenly a hand touched hers and a voice said, "Hey, Dixie, come out of it!"

Dixie's eyes flew open, and she whirled to see Ollie Peck standing at the truck door and grinning at her. He was wearing a pair of faded jeans and a disreputable-looking T-shirt with a picture of an alligator on it.

"What is the alligator for?" she asked.

"Aw, we were down in Florida, and we went to an alligator farm. I tried to get Dad to let me bring home a *real* alligator, but he wouldn't do it."

"I don't think alligators would be very

good pets. Or any kind of reptile!" Dixie said.

"Why, some people keep snakes for pets."

"I know it, but I wouldn't want to have one around me. I don't like snakes."

Ollie grinned at her. He reached in and pulled her hair, not hard, just teasing her. "You remember the time I put a green snake in your lunch box?" His eyes sparkled, and he laughed aloud. "That was an interesting lunch for you that day!"

Dixie tried to get angry but she could not. "If you ever do that again," she said, holding back a smile, "I'll do something worse than that to you!"

As they were talking and laughing together, Patty and Leslie Stone came out of the drugstore. Seeing Ollie talking to Dixie, they both came over to the pickup.

"Hi, Dixie, what are you doing?" Patty asked.

"Just came to town to get Uncle Roy a haircut and some groceries."

"I think it's about time we had another sleepover," Patty said. She was always in favor of sleepovers. "We can have one at my house again."

107

"No, we've done that twice already," Dixie said. "Let's make it *my* house." She suddenly looked at Leslie, who had not even greeted her and was frowning slightly. She made herself smile and said, "You can come, can't you, Leslie? It'll just be the three of us."

Leslie hesitated. "I guess so," she said.

"Good! Let's do it Monday night."

"Don't you have to ask your aunt?"

"Oh, she won't mind. She says she likes the company. She gets bored sitting in that wheelchair."

At that moment a truck went by, and Ollie glanced up. "There's Neil Sparks," he said. "He's got some more coons, it looks like. He must be making a fortune."

Patty nodded. "I think he is. Daddy said they pay him so much a coon, and then he dresses them out and sells the hides and the meat besides."

Leslie was looking at Dixie's face and must have seen the anger that came into her eyes. "You still don't like it, do you, Dixie? Trapping the coons? But it has to be done. They're pests. You don't worry about killing roaches, do you?"

Dixie knew that Leslie was trying to make her mad. She merely said, "I don't know. It seems like there's a difference between roaches and raccoons. Roaches are dirty, and coons are very clean. Why, they wash a lot of what they eat."

"I didn't know you were such an expert on coons," Leslie said. Then she took Ollie's arm. "Come on, Ollie. Patty and I were just going to get some ice cream."

"Are you buying?" Ollie said.

"Yes, I am."

"Good! I never turn down free ice cream." Ollie turned to go but then asked, "You coming, Dixie?"

Dixie actually wanted to go. She would have if it had been only Ollie and Patty. But she said, "No, I have to wait for Uncle Roy. He'll be back from the barbershop soon." Then she said to the girls, "You two come on over about four o'clock, Monday. You can help me fix supper. We can fix anything we want."

Patty grinned and said, "How about chocolate pie, coconut cake, and blueberry cobbler for dessert?"

"You'd be fat as a pig!" Dixie said. "But we'll fix something good."

The three went off, and Dixie felt a little lonely. She was pleased when Kelly

Stone came along. As he was passing the truck, not seeing her, she said, "Hello, Kelly, are you looking for Leslie?"

Kelly was wearing a pair of khaki pants and a blue shirt. He had the bluest eyes Dixie had ever seen. Now he grinned and walked over to the pickup door. "Yes, have you seen her?"

"She went with Ollie and Patty to have some ice cream."

"Well, what's holding *you* back? Have you given up ice cream?"

"No, but I have to get on home."

Then Kelly said, "Are you going back to the circus soon?"

"I don't think so. Not soon. Not until Aunt Edith is able to take care of herself."

"Well, we haven't seen much of you lately, but there's going to be a hayride at the church tomorrow night. Seven o'clock."

"Why, I'd like to come to that."

"Good! We'll have a great time! We always have a good time on those hayrides."

While Kelly continued to talk happily about the hayride, Dixie was watching Neil Sparks display his catch of coons to an admiring group over in front of the sheriff's office. She didn't want to see any of the coons. It always made her sad.

At last Uncle Roy appeared with his hair cut too short, as usual.

"You got your hair cut too short!"

"I don't tell you how to do *your* hair." Uncle Roy grinned. "And you don't tell me how to do my hair." He got inside the truck and started it.

Dixie said, "I'll see you later, Kelly."

"Yeah, don't forget about the hayride."

The truck rattled out of town, and when they got to the house Uncle Roy started to take the groceries in. "Well, you sure went overboard on dog food."

Dixie could not say a word for a minute. The coons were eating so much, it was the best thing she could think of to feed them. She always bought it with her own money, however, and didn't take it out of the grocery money for the household.

"I thought—I thought we'd just keep some on hand. It'll be eaten sooner or later."

"Shep will be as big around as Jumbo if he eats all this."

The sleepover was not a success.
Both girls helped cook supper as Dixie

had suggested. She showed them how to make meatloaf, which was another of her favorite dishes. "It's real easy," she said. "Here's all you do . . ."

She took down a large bowl and began crumbling bread crumbs and chopping onions, green pepper, and a clove of garlic. She added half a cup of tomato sauce and mixed these together. She added a pound and a half of ground beef and a half pound of ground pork. Dixie then slightly beat two eggs with a fork, added some salt and pepper, then poured them into the larger bowl. She looked at the mixture, then dove in with her hands to mix all of the ingredients together.

"You sure do like to cook, don't you, Dixie?" Patty said.

"I think it's fun."

"When I get married, I'm going to have a *cook* so I don't have to do any of that," Leslie said. "And then I'll have a maid to take care of all my clothes."

"You better marry a rich man then," Patty said.

"I'm going to."

The three girls washed and dried the dishes—or rather, Patty and Dixie did, while Leslie mostly stood and watched. When that chore was done, they adjourned to the farmhouse living room, where they watched a scary television program.

"I don't know what the world's coming to," Uncle Roy said. He sat in his chair eating Hershey's Kisses for dessert, even though Dixie had made brownies. He stared at the screen.

"I don't think it's healthy for you to watch such things," Aunt Edith said.

"Oh, it's just all in fun, Aunt Edith," Dixie protested. "Nobody really believes in ghosts and things like that."

"Well, I'm about to," Uncle Roy said, frowning. "Never saw so many things missing. Every time I look for something, it's gone. I believe we've got some kind of a thief around here."

Candy hadn't taken the coons to the woods yet, and Dixie knew they were getting into things on the porch or in the yard. She didn't answer Uncle Roy's comment.

After the program, the three girls got ready to go upstairs.

"I'll turn all the lights out after you go to bed," Dixie said to her aunt and uncle. "We'll see you in the morning."

"Don't you make too much racket up there," Uncle Roy said.

"We won't. Good night." She went over and kissed Uncle Roy and Aunt Edith, and her two companions bade them good night.

Upstairs, they played music for a while, but Leslie didn't like the same kind of music that Dixie and Patty did. She insisted on playing a CD that she had brought with her. It was a wild rock recording, and Patty said, "I bet your folks don't know you're playing music like that, Leslie!"

"There's nothing wrong with this music!" Leslie said defensively.

Dixie said, "It's the words to rock music that can be pretty bad."

"I don't know about that!" Leslie sniffed. "I just like the beat!"

They took turns playing the two different kinds of music, then finally played Nintendo. Dixie had gotten a new one recently, and all three enjoyed that.

Finally they showered and got into their pajamas, but no one was sleepy. Dixie's small TV played videos, and they stayed up watching a Shirley Temple movie and then *The Lion King* again.

Finally Patty and Leslie drifted off to sleep.

Dixie got up quietly, put on her slippers, and went downstairs. Her aunt and uncle had gone to bed a long time ago.

She found Bandit and the cubs all waiting when she brought out the dog food, the grapes, and the M&M's. Sitting down, she fed them and, as always, enjoyed their antics. The cubs were fat and roly-poly now from eating no one knew how many pounds of dog food.

"You're the cutest things I've ever seen!" she whispered.

They fell down and rolled over and pretended to bite and scratch. They scrambled and played and chased each other but were not agile like cats. Dixie kept sitting there on the steps in the moonlight, watching.

Finally she whispered, "You be very quiet tonight now. I don't want to hear anything out of you."

But if Dixie had looked up, she would have seen that she had a spectator. Leslie Stone was leaning out the window and staring down at what was happening. She watched until Dixie shooed the coons off and they disappeared, and then a strange smile came to her lips.

"Well, so this is what you're doing!" she whispered. Then she got back into bed and pretended to be asleep, but she did not forget what she had seen.

After the church service the following Sunday morning, Sheriff Peck came up to Dixie. "You got a minute, Dixie?"

She was surprised but went with him out to the side of the church, where people were getting into their cars.

"I think we've got a little problem, Dixie."

"Problem? What kind of problem, Sheriff Peck?"

"I got a report I have to talk to you about."

Dixie's heart suddenly sank. She somehow knew what was coming. "What is it, Sheriff?"

"Well, I can't reveal my sources, but I know that you are keeping some coons out at your place. That's a real problem."

Instantly Dixie knew that it was Leslie who had informed on her. She exclaimed, "That Leslie Stone! She told you, didn't she?"

"I can't tell you where I got my information. Dixie, if your uncle and aunt lived outside the city limits, it wouldn't matter. But the town has taken in the area that their house is on, so now the city ordinances apply there."

"Those coons aren't doing any harm!"

"Do your uncle and aunt know they're there?"

Dixie suddenly blushed a little. "No, sir, they don't."

"I didn't think so. Well, Dixie, you're going to have to do something about it."

"But they're not hurting anybody! I feed them, and I pay for the food with my own money!"

"Others have not agreed with this new ordinance, either," the sheriff said. He shrugged his beefy shoulders. "I don't agree with it myself, but it's the law now, and we have to keep the law."

Dixie stood silently for a while, and then she said, "Are you going to tell that awful man who traps them?"

Sheriff Peck put his hands on Dixie's shoulder. "I don't want to have to do that, Dixie. I think you should handle this yourself."

"I can't tell *him!* He'd take them and kill them, and I love them, Sheriff Peck!"

The sheriff looked uncomfortable. He probably did not like Neil Sparks, either. "Well, I'm not going to tell you what to do. All I can say is, what you're doing is dangerous."

"They're not dangerous! They never hurt anybody!" she protested.

"I don't mean that. I mean deceiving your aunt and your uncle is dangerous. Deceiving is never good. I think you need to start by going and telling them. They're very good folks, and I expect they can help you with this problem."

Dixie knew there was no way out. "All right, Sheriff. I'll tell them."

When she left Sheriff Peck, Dixie was boiling inside. "That Leslie Stone! It had to be her! Somehow she saw the coons when she and Patty stayed all night with me! I hate her! It's none of her business how many coons are at our house!"

Dixie Morris was as angry as she had ever been in her life. She knew it was wrong to feel that way, but she could not help it. All the way home from church, she had to keep her lips tightly pressed together. She was simmering.

10
DIXIE DECIDES

Try as she might and even though she'd promised, Dixie still couldn't bring herself to tell her uncle and aunt about the coons. She had thought of every possible way to tell them, but—no matter what she thought—she just couldn't come out and do it.

They'd think they'd have to tell that old Sparks man, she said to herself, *and then he'd come and get all the coons!*

After a week, Dixie was out of dog food again, and she had no money to get any more.

That afternoon when Candy was going to town to get more supplies in the pickup, Dixie said, "Candy, do you have any money?"

"Sure."

"Will you lend me some?"

"OK. How much do you want?"

Dixie knew she had to trust someone. "All I want is two sacks of dog food—and, Candy, I'd just as soon Aunt Edith and Uncle Roy not know about it."

Candy looked down at her. He was a very big man, and Dixie always felt small beside him. He asked quietly, "Is it for the coons?"

"Yes, it is," she said. "Oh, Candy, Sheriff Peck knows about them, and he says something's got to be done." Then Dixie burst out, "It was that old Leslie Stone that told on me! I hate her, Candy!"

Candy looked down at the girl. He suddenly put his hand on her head and smoothed her long, blonde hair. "Come on over to the barn," he said, "and we'll talk about it."

He led her out to the barn, and they sat on a bale of hay. Candy began to talk. Dixie was surprised, for he did not say much, as a rule. Finally he said, "Everybody has problems they got to solve, Dixie. Grown-ups too. Just growing up is a hard thing."

Dixie looked up at him, and asked, "Did you have a hard time growing up?"

"Well, I don't know," Candy said. He ran his hand over his sandy hair and shook his head. "My folks died when I was only four—in an automobile wreck. I got passed around to different relatives. I wasn't very smart. I didn't do too well in school. The kids always made fun of me. But that was all right. Then I got a job here with your uncle and aunt, and they're good to me."

Dixie had never known about Candy's childhood. She felt sorry for him. She took his huge hand and held it in both of hers. "I'm sorry you had such a hard time, Candy. I've mostly had an easy time myself."

"Well, I'm glad for that. Now, I know if your mom and dad was here, they'd tell you what to do. I can't tell you—except you have to do what's right."

"You think it's wrong not to tell Neil Sparks about the coons."

"I think there's something else maybe as bad as that."

"What's that, Candy?"

"Well, ever since I met you last summer, Dixie, I always thought you was the sweetest girl in the world. And now I see how mad you are at the preacher's daughter."

"Well, she's a tattletale!"

Candy's innocent, blue eyes rested on Dixie. He squeezed her hands with his big one and said, "Lots of people do things we don't like. But like I told you, that's her problem. *Your* problem is what you're going to do about it. If you get mad at her, that only hurts you."

Dixie remembered that Candy had said this to her before. He himself was a very gentle man and never seemed to get angry at anyone. "So what do you really think I ought to do, Candy?"

He was quiet for a long time. He lifted his eyes and looked out into the gathering darkness. Finally, he shook his head. "I guess you know, Dixie, that coons are wild animals. They're not like cats and dogs."

"Bandit and her babies seem tame to me! They're so playful and—"

"I know they seem that way now. Especially the little ones. But if you try to cage 'em and keep 'em like a cat or a dog, it doesn't work. I've known half a dozen people try to make pets out of coons. They're cute when they're little, but sooner or later they've got to go back into the wild. That's just the way they are. It's the way God made 'em, I reckon. They're different from cats and dogs."

Dixie sat there listening as Candy continued to explain the way coons were. He finished by saying, "They *can't* be tamed, Dixie. Ever. You'll lose them, anyhow, when they get older."

"I didn't know all that, Candy," she whispered.

"You know what I think?"

"What do you think?"

"I think you ought to pray about how to do this. I think both of us should. Let's me and you pray that God will get you out of this trouble. And especially that He'll help you do what's right—and that means being honest with your aunt and uncle and doing the right thing about them coons."

Suddenly Dixie felt better. "I'm glad to have a friend like you, Candy. You've always been so good to me. I remember if I hadn't had you to help with Jumbo, I don't think we could have saved him."

The two prayed together, very quietly, and then Dixie said, "I know what I've got to do, Candy. I guess I've always known."

"What are you going to do?"

"First, I'm going to tell Uncle Roy and

Aunt Edith about the coons. Right now. And tomorrow I'm going to Sheriff Peck and tell him that I'm going to keep the law, whatever that is."

"Dixie, that's good." Candy was silent for a moment. "It'd be hard for you to see that fellow come and trap these coons. I hope it don't happen. Maybe there's a way out."

"Well, I'm asking the Lord to help me —and the coons too. I even named them, Candy."

"What did you name them?"

Dixie smiled. "I named the mama Bandit, but I guess her name should be Bandita. And I named the baby coons after the apostles, Simon, Andrew, James, John, and Nathaniel."

"I thought there was twelve of them."

"Well—" Dixie smiled "—I guess I ran out of coons."

11

TROUBLE FOR BANDIT AND COMPANY

Immediately after talking with Candy, Dixie went inside and found her uncle and aunt watching the news on television. She waited until it was over and then said, "Can I turn the TV off? I've got something to tell you."

And then Dixie told them the whole story. She ended by saying, "I'm so sorry that I didn't tell you before. I was wrong not to. I was afraid you wouldn't like it."

"Why, I never troubled myself over a thing like coons around the place," Roy said with surprise. "There's always a coon or a possum around. But still, it wasn't smart to get close to 'em like that, Dixie. Any one of 'em can bite, and they can carry disease."

Aunt Edith was studying Dixie's face.

She asked gently, "You've really been upset about this, haven't you, honey?"

"Yes, I have, Aunt Edith. I guess being around animals in the circus has made me love them more. But I was so wrong to deceive you. And it was dumb of me to risk getting bit—I know that now. And I understand now that coons are *wild* animals— Candy says they all go back to the wild anyway. But I just couldn't stand the thought of Neil Sparks killing them."

An angry look flashed into Uncle Roy's eyes, and his face flushed. "Still, I don't see as it's any of Neil Sparks's business how many coons I have!"

"You remember, Roy," Aunt Edith said, "the city council passed that ordinance."

"And Fred Smith was behind that! I heard all about it! It's none of his business, either!"

"Well, it's the law," her aunt said, "and now we've got to do something about keeping it."

"I'm going in tomorrow and tell Sheriff Peck that he can do whatever he has to do," Dixie said quietly. She cried a little and said, "But I don't think I could stand it if anything happens to Simon and Andrew and the rest."

"Simon and Andrew—oh, that's what you named the coons?"

"Yes, after five of the apostles."

"You know, it's strange," Aunt Edith said, "how once you put a name to something, you get attached to it. If I just saw a coon out on the road, I wouldn't think anything about it. But if one came around the house, I'd get attached to it and probably name it."

"That's what I did, Aunt Edith," Dixie said eagerly, "and they're such good animals. I mean, they have been . . ."

"Well, we'll see how it comes out," Uncle Roy said. "Don't worry about it too much, Dixie. Things like this have a way of working themselves out."

The next day Dixie rode into town with Candy. "Take me by the sheriff's office first. I've got to tell him before I lose my nerve."

He stopped the pickup in front of the office and said, "I'll wait for you out here."

"All right, Candy."

Going inside, Dixie found Sheriff Peck behind his desk. She marched up to him and held her head high. "Sheriff, you were right about the coons. I've come to tell you that you can do whatever has to be done."

Sheriff Peck looked surprised. He put down his ballpoint pen and stood up. Then he came around the desk and looked down at her.

"I've got to keep the law, Sheriff Peck. You were right, and Candy was right, too."

Sheriff Peck suddenly smiled. "I'm sorry about the coons, but I'm happy about the way you're handling it, Dixie. Not many youngsters could do this kind of thing."

Dixie nodded but could feel a lump in her throat. "Do you think he'll do it soon? Trap the coons, I mean."

"I guess he will." Sheriff Peck shook his head. "I never liked that fella, but I guess he'll do what he's been hired to do."

Dixie left the sheriff's office. Out on the street she found Candy waiting in the truck.

"Did you tell him?" he asked.

"Yes, I did."

Candy looked closely at her. "Come on," he said. "Let's go get some ice cream."

"I don't want any."

"I bet you will when you see what I order."

Candy got out of the truck, and Dixie followed him. He took her small hand in his large one, and they went to the TCBY. There, Candy winked at her, saying, "Let's have two banana splits."

Dixie smiled up at the big man. She knew he was trying to make things easier for her. "Thank you, Candy. But I don't think I can eat a whole one."

At that moment Kelly Stone came in. "I saw you come over here. Is it time for ice cream?"

"Sure," Candy said. "And it's on me. Order anything you want."

"Anything? It might break you up, Candy."

"Go right ahead. Anything you want."

"What are you having, Dixie?"

"Well, a banana split, but you can have half of it. I can never eat a whole one."

"That sounds great to me. Can I pick out some of the flavors?"

"You can pick them all out."

Dixie watched as Kelly ordered the ice cream, and they sat down at a table.

Candy ate his banana split quickly. "You two can sit here and talk. I got to go see about gettin' the oil changed in the truck. I'll pick you up here after while, Dixie, or you can come over to the garage."

"All right, Candy."

When Candy was gone, Kelly continued to eat from his end of the banana split bowl. "Sure is good," he said.

But Dixie had stopped eating.

He glanced at her and said, "I guess you're not feeling too good about the coons."

Dixie looked up. "How did you know about that?"

A disgusted look swept over Kelly's face. "Leslie told me what she did. We had a real row about it! I ought to sock her!"

"She told you that she went to Sheriff Peck?"

"Yeah, she did, and she was proud of it. I was disgusted!" Kelly was not too disgusted to eat, however. He took another huge bite of banana. "And then she made the mistake of telling Dad about it. Boy, you should have heard what he told her!"

"What did he say, Kelly?"

"Well, I hope he never talks to me like he talked to her. He told her she was a tattletale, and he said the Bible calls that a 'talebearer.' I just told her she was wrong, but Dad made her cry."

"He did? I can't imagine that!"

"Well, Leslie's a funny kid. She's not bad. She's spoiled, of course. Everybody knows that. And she does things to call attention to herself."

Dixie sat there, staring at him. She finally said, "How did it all come out?"

"Oh, she got grounded, and she cried all day. And then, somehow word got out, and now everybody's mad at her for being a stool pigeon."

Kelly ate the rest of the banana split. When Dixie got up to go to the garage, he said, "You don't have to worry about getting even with Leslie. She's about as miserable as I ever saw her."

"I don't want to get even with her," Dixie said.

But as she left the ice cream parlor, she was thinking, *At first I did want to get even with her! I was so mad I could've pulled all her hair out!* But now Dixie was thinking about one thing: *How would I feel if I had done something really wrong, and my dad had been so mad at me?*

She remembered a few occasions when this had happened. Her father, as much as he loved Dixie, could be stern about some things. Dixie could remember his taking her on his lap and talking with her about things she had done wrong. It had always ended with her crying bitterly. But then he had always comforted her. Putting his arms around her, he would tell her he loved her and that it was only for her own good that he was saying these things.

At the garage, Dixie got into the pickup with Candy, and the two drove home. Candy said nothing. Dixie was thinking deeply all the way.

When they reached the house, they both got out, and Dixie said, "Thanks for taking me, Candy."

"It's OK." He hesitated, then said, "I'm afraid it's going to be pretty bad. About the coons, I mean."

"I guess so. But there's one thing—I'm not going to be mad at Leslie anymore."

Candy's face rolled into a large grin. He came around the truck and gave her a hug. "That's good, Dixie. Never good to stay mad at anybody."

Dixie gave her uncle and aunt a report of her visit to the sheriff, and then she began cleaning the house. She was vacu-uming the living-room rug when the doorbell rang. She turned off the vacuum and went to the door.

Leslie Stone was standing on the porch.

"Why, Leslie," Dixie said, "come on in."

"No, I can't, but will you come out? I—I have something to tell you."

"Sure." Dixie stepped outside. She saw that Leslie's eyes were red. She had obviously been crying. She saw also that the older girl was twisting her fingers together nervously.

"I came to tell you—" Leslie could not finish, and fresh tears came into her eyes. Then she sobbed and said, "I came to tell you how sorry I am about what I did. I wish I hadn't done it. Will you forgive me?"

Dixie immediately lost every bit of resentment that remained. She knew exactly what Leslie was going through, for she had been there herself. "It's all right, Leslie," she said quickly. "It's all over now."

"You're not mad at me?"

"Not anymore. I was," Dixie said, "but we all make mistakes. And now we can go on from here. Don't cry."

Leslie wiped her eyes with the back of her hands and sniffled a little. Then she said, "I feel so awful. Daddy talked to me about how bad it is to be a talebearer."

"I feel exactly the same way when I do something I shouldn't and my dad talks to *me*. Can't keep from crying," Dixie said. "We learn something, and that's good. But it hurts at the time."

"I don't know what made me do it. I guess I'm just terrible."

"No, you're not terrible. You're one of the prettiest, smartest girls I ever saw. You just made a mistake."

"Well, I'll never make *that* mistake again." Then Leslie said, "I know you love those coons. I'm not much of an animal lover, but I'll help you any way I can. Can we kidnap them and hide them from that awful Neil Sparks?"

"No, that wouldn't be right, I'm afraid."

"Well, we've got to do something."

"I don't think there's anything to do," Dixie said.

"There's got to be a way. I'll tell you what—let's all of us get together, and maybe we'll think of something. Me and you, and Kelly, and Ollie, and Patty . . ."

Dixie did not see how that would help, but she agreed.

Late that afternoon, the five of them gathered in Dixie's room. Leslie looked a little bit sheepish, and Dixie knew that the others had spoken harshly to her about what she had done.

As soon as they were inside, she put an arm around Leslie. "Leslie's told me how sorry she is about what she did—and once anybody does that, it's all over." She hugged the girl hard and said, "OK, Leslie?"

Leslie looked around nervously. "Yes, I guess so. But I still wish we could do something about the coons."

For a long time they sat there, talking and trying to think of a way to save the raccoon family.

Ollie thought he had a simple solution. "Let's each take one or two of the babies home with us. It'll be easier to hide one or two than it would five."

"That won't do," Dixie said. "That's the mistake I've been making all along. We *can't* keep them. It wouldn't be right to hide them."

Kelly said, "Let's go out in the woods and build a cage, and we can keep them there until it all blows over."

"Not going to blow over," Dixie said

sadly. "It's the law. We've got to face up to the truth."

After a long time, Patty said, "I can't think of anything we can do, but God can help us. He saved Jonah in the lions' den, didn't He?"

"It wasn't Jonah! He was in the whale's belly!" But Dixie smiled. "It was Daniel who was in the lions' den."

"Whatever! He saved lots of folks in the Bible. Surely He can save a bunch of baby coons. Let's just pray about it."

And that was what they did. Dixie was hoping that God would give her a good feeling about the coons then. But as the others left, she had to make herself smile and say, "It'll be all right somehow."

That night, however, when she fed Bandita and all of her babies, great sadness came over her. All she could think was, *Neil Sparks is going to get you, and none of you will be alive anymore.*

12

TO THE RESCUE

I saw that Sparks fellow in town this morning. He's coming out to trap the coons."

When Dixie looked up quickly from her oatmeal, she saw that Uncle Roy and Aunt Edith were looking at her strangely. She said nothing but suddenly lost her appetite.

"Don't worry about it, honey. Maybe things will be all right."

Dixie knew that things would not be all right, and all day she was very sad. Candy had heard the news, too, and he tried to cheer her up. But nothing anybody said actually made much difference.

Late that afternoon, Neil Sparks's truck pulled up. "Well, I've come to trap the coons," he said. He was smiling, but he also had an unpleasant look on his face. "Though I guess you know where they are, don't you?"

"They're out in the barn."

"Well, that'll make it easier." He laughed then and said, "You put one over on me, but I don't hold it against you. But I got to do my job."

"Then just go on and do it!" Uncle Roy had come out, his face red. "Get on with it and be quiet about it, Neil Sparks!"

"What are you so huffy about?" Sparks asked.

"You heard me! Now get on with it!"

Sparks stared at the older man, then muttered, "Don't know what's eatin' on you," but he went toward the barn and disappeared inside to set his traps.

He came out soon, saying, "I put some real good bait in those traps. They'll all be in 'em pretty soon."

He drove off, still laughing, and Dixie could hardly bear to think about all of her babies being in Neil Sparks's traps. She walked away quickly and stayed by herself out in the woods the rest of the afternoon.

When she came back, she saw that Sparks had returned and was taking the traps out of the barn. She also saw Leslie,

Kelly, Ollie, and Patty standing on the porch.

They all ran to greet her, and all of them looked sad.

"Isn't there anything we can do?" Ollie asked.

"Nothing I know of," Dixie said. For a while she stood watching, and then said, "I've got to go say good-bye to Bandita and the babies." When she went out to the truck, she saw that all three traps were filled and that all of the coons were pawing at the wire cages.

"Better say good-bye, girl," Neil Sparks said. He leaned against the truck and began to pick his teeth with a toothpick.

Candy Sweet came up. He towered over the smaller man. Candy said very softly, "Don't say anything."

"What?" Sparks looked up at the enormous man and swallowed hard. "What did you say?"

"I said," Candy repeated quietly, "don't say anything!"

"Well, I wasn't going to," Sparks said. He started to get into his truck, but Candy reached out and pushed him back. "You wait. I'll tell you when you can go."

Dixie tried to keep the tears back but could not. Although the coons may have looked alike to the others, she knew each one of them. "Good-bye, Simon. Good-bye, Andrew." She went around and touched each cage. Then she turned away and could not help but sob. She went to Uncle Roy, and he put his arms around her and held her.

Neil Sparks shot a cautious look at Candy. Seeing the big man still standing nearby, Sparks tried to be more assertive. "Well, it's all over. I'll be gettin' out of here now—"

At that moment a red vehicle suddenly appeared over the rise.

Uncle Roy said, "Don't know that truck. Sure is a fancy one, though."

"It's one of them Dodge Rams with four doors," Candy said.

The strange red truck did not go by. Instead, it stopped directly in front of the gate.

Dixie was too overcome with grief to pay much attention, but then the door slammed, and she heard her name called.

"Hey, Dixie!"

Dixie wiped her eyes and looked at the

tall boy who had gotten out of the truck and was running toward her. "Chad!" she cried and ran to meet him.

Chad Taylor—he would be sixteen now—had dark hair and the darkest eyes in the world. He was wearing a pair of faded jeans and a big belt buckle, cowboy boots, and a cowboy shirt. He had a Stetson on his head, which he took off and tossed on the ground before grabbing Dixie and whirling her around.

"How you doing?"

"Chad, where did you come from?"

"All the way from Arkansas. How do you like my new truck?"

Dixie did not even look at the truck. She was very fond of her friend Chad. Together the two of them had saved Jumbo, the elephant, from being put to sleep. She clung to him and said, "I'm so glad to see you. But it's a sad time."

Chad set her down, then put his hand on her blonde hair. "What are you crying about?"

Dixie started to talk. "It's my coons. I love them, and that man's going to take them and—"

Chad Taylor looked over at the group

beside Neil Sparks's truck. Then his jaw hardened. He grabbed Dixie's hand and marched toward them, saying, "What's going on here? What about these coons?"

Neil Sparks said, "City ordinance says I'm supposed to take all the coons out of the city limits, and that's what I aim to do."

"He's going to kill them!" Dixie could not help saying. "*That's* what he's going to do! And they're so sweet, and they're not hurting anybody."

"The law says they have to go," Sparks said.

"I'm afraid that's right," Uncle Roy put in.

Chad Taylor looked at Dixie's face and bent down to whisper in her ear, "You like these coons, Dixie?"

"Yes, I do. I love them very much. They're tame—well, almost. They like to sleep in our barn."

Then Chad said to Neil Sparks, "I don't know your name, mister, but I can save you some trouble." He picked up the cage containing two of the baby coons and set it on the ground.

"Hey, what you doing? Leave those cages alone!"

"I'll take care of the coons for you," Chad said coolly.

"You can't do that! I'm authorized to get rid of them!"

Chad was a strongly built boy, and when he stood in front of Neil Sparks, he too loomed over the raccoon trapper. "I said I'll get rid of the coons for you. You don't need to bother. I'll give you your cages, and you can be on your way! Anybody here want to help me set these coons loose?"

Uncle Roy grabbed a cage, and Candy grabbed another. Soon all the coons were loose. At once, they all made for the barn.

"Don't guess we need to detain you anymore, Sparks," Candy said. "Here are your cages. You can be on your way."

"I'm gonna have Sheriff Peck out here! You'll be arrested, whoever you are!"

"Be looking forward to seeing the sheriff. I know him well. You tell him Chad Taylor's here and he's taking these coons all the way back to Arkansas to the best coon country in the world."

"Oh, Chad, can you do that?" Dixie cried, staring up at him with her mouth open.

"Don't see why not. My uncle—L. G. Taylor—he owns three thousand acres of woods, and these coons won't make much difference in there. They'll have a good home, too."

Neil Sparks began to mutter, but he picked up the empty cages and threw them into his truck. Then he got in and drove off, shouting, "I'll have the law on you, you'll see!"

Dixie turned to Chad and gave him a hug. "Can you really do that? Take them to Arkansas and see that they have a good home?"

"Sure can, and they'll have good company too." He laughed. "They can visit with Jumbo. And when you come to visit, we might be able to find one or two of these little ring-tailed fellows for you. Don't you worry, Dixie. I'll see they're safe."

Dixie looked around at her friends and saw that everyone was smiling. She took a deep breath and said, "Now, things will really be all right. Bandita and her babies will be safe."

"I guess we ought to have a celebration," Candy said. "Let's go down and get some ice cream."

And that is what they did.

As they piled out of Uncle Roy's truck in front of the ice cream parlor, Dixie saw Neil Sparks across the street, waving his arms and talking excitedly with the sheriff.

But Sheriff Peck was laughing. He turned and came over to Chad and the other new arrivals. "Well, you're sure growing up, Chad. It's good to see you again."

"Good to see you too, Sheriff. Did that fellow over there tell you what a terrible criminal I was?"

"He tried to. What's this all about?"

"Why, I drove down for a visit with Dixie and her folks. I'm taking all these coons back to Arkansas with me. No trouble at all to have over there."

Dixie put an arm around Chad. "Isn't that wonderful, Sheriff? God sent him just in time. I think he's just like an angel."

Chad Taylor laughed. He was a handsome boy with long black hair and sparkling black eyes. "Been called lots of things, but never that. Come on now. Let's go inside and celebrate. Sheriff, won't you join us?"

"I believe I will." Sheriff Peck reached over, stroked Dixie's hair, and smiled down at her. "It looks like your coons are safe."

"Yes," Dixie said. "The Lord did find a good way to take care of them. But then, He always does things right." She looked around at her friends and said, "We're all going to remember that, aren't we? Now, let's go in and eat all the ice cream we can."